DARKNESS WITHIN THE FOREST

MATTHEW NEIGHBOURS

Darkness Within the Forest / Matthew Neighbours
ISBN: 978-0-9986525-2-8
Cover art by Damonza

CONTENTS

CHAPTER 1 1

CHAPTER 2 15

CHAPTER 3 29

CHAPTER 4 39

CHAPTER 5 53

CHAPTER 6 81

CHAPTER 7 101

CHAPTER 8 113

CHAPTER 9 143

CHAPTER 10 157

CHAPTER 11 173

CHAPTER 12 179

CHAPTER 13 185

CHAPTER 14 189

CHAPTER 15 199

CHAPTER 16 211

CHAPTER 17 217

CHAPTER 18 223

CHAPTER 19 229

CHAPTER 20 245

CHAPTER 21 263

2 WEEKS LATER 279

CHAPTER 1

James downed the rest of his coffee, tossing the empty Styrofoam cup onto the floor of the passenger side, rubbing his eyes. The last two days had been a drunken blur as he sought to suppress thought, spending nights drifting in and out of sleep, consumed by the constant memories that he struggled to banish from his mind. His head was pounding, and there was a dryness in his throat that the coffee wasn't doing much to dissipate.

It was three nights ago when he had driven up here to Anchorage, though he remembered little of it now. A quick glance at the dashboard informed him it was 9:54 a.m. James held his hand out horizontally before him—it was shaking uncontrollably. There was a tingling across his skin and his head was buzzing from the several cups of coffee he had consumed to waken from his troubled sleep, but mostly there was the anticipation of finally receiving some kind of information, and the opportunity of getting to talk to the detective.

He stepped out of the car and looked at the large square glass building, about six stories high, which was the Anchorage Police Department, situated right up against the street in the middle of the downtown area.

James looked at a bar and a souvenir shop directly across the road, seeing a little girl pulling ahead of her parents eagerly pointing toward a food truck at the intersection. An elderly couple were looking over a brochure, likely discussing some attraction they could go to later and planning out their day. The sidewalks were beginning to fill with tourists, people eager to explore what the city offered and going about their daily lives.

He stuttered his name out to the receptionist at the front desk, furtively glancing at the large police shield painted on the wall behind her, then swept his gaze toward the clock, almost jumping when the young girl told him to have a seat and wait. It seemed oppressively hot as he sat there in the lobby, absently pulling at a loose string at the hem of his shirt. Ten minutes later, a man entered the area and called James to follow him. He had medium short graying hair that was hastily tossed to the side and was wearing a white shirt with a loose tie that was cocked to the left. The hallway they were walking down seemed to go on and on as they passed by many offices and cubicles before the man in front of James finally entered his own small office. This was the first time meeting the man now in front of him, as James had spoken to a different detective on that previous morning.

"Thank you for coming back in, James. I'm Detective Aiden Smith, homicide," the man said as he shook James's hand. "Take a seat."

Homicide. His entire body seemed to lock up for a moment as the word sent a shock throughout his senses. He knew he shouldn't have such a reaction, because who should he be speaking to if not a homicide detective? The man seemed to sink behind his desk as he sat down. He appeared to be somewhere in his forties, and the lines in his face told of his many years in this occupation, which had now taken its weary toll on him.

"As I informed you when we talked over the phone, I'll be taking over the case now." Detective Smith took a sip of coffee from a mug with an APD logo on it before placing it back down next to an old and grubby fedora. "I've been going over the transcripts of your interview, and there are a few points I want to go back over, just to make sure I have everything straight."

"Yes... That's fine." James's head was pounding again as he felt a wave of discouragement move through him. *This is okay, it's just protocol. Let him ask a few questions, and then I will get the answers I came here for.* He took a few deep breaths trying to calm his nerves.

"Again, there are a few facts I need to get straight." The detective shuffled some papers about his desk. He arched an eyebrow, looking up at James. "You said that she *did* take her own life, correct?"

"Elena? Yes technically, but—"

"And you saw all this happen yourself?" the detective asked, cutting him off.

"Yeah, but as I told the other detective—"

"Yes, yes, it's all in the transcripts and we'll get to all of that," Smith said, interrupting him again. "Let's see now. She didn't have any identification on her, but a fingerprint match came back. Elena Eckridge, twenty-four-years old, born in Homer Alaska, last known address was here in Anchorage."

Elena Eckridge. For the first time, he realized he had never known her last name. The veins in his neck and temples strained against his skin at this minor revelation, and he could feel his pulse rising. This brought the question which had been ever pressing upon his mind over the last two days to the forefront of his thoughts. "Did you talk to him? What did he say? Did you arrest him?"

Detective Smith raised his hand to stop him. "Let's back up for a minute." He took another sip of coffee. "Would you like a cup of coffee?" he offered.

"No, I don't need any damn coff... sorry." James stopped, breathing in deeply as he tried to ease his agitation. "A coffee would be great, thank you."

The detective grabbed the pot of coffee which was tucked into the office's corner and filled a Styrofoam cup before sitting at his desk again. "I wanted to ask, why did you drive all the way up here that night, instead of going to the much closer Seward Police Station, or simply call 911, once you had cell reception?"

"I... don't... I just don't know. That night's still blurry to me. I just had to get out of there, and I think I thought about how small the Seward PD must be, and that you would have a lot more resources up here to handle the case. And what good would calling 911 be if I was just heading over here, anyway? There wasn't an active emergency any longer at that point."

"Okay, fair enough, so getting back to your interview. You say the first time you met her, Elena, was when she—what was it you said exactly," he looked through several pages of paper, the transcript of James's previous conversation with the other detective. "Ah yes, 'she jumped into the ocean from a cliff.'" Smith looked right at James now. "And it was just a coincidence that you were there when this happened?"

"Yes, that's right," James said, ignoring the sarcasm in the detective's voice and trying to keep the desperation he was feeling out of his own words. "But like I said before, it wasn't coincidence at all in the—"

"I know, it's all right here," he tapped his fingers on the papers laying across his desk. "So, you jumped in to save her life, and then brought her to the house you were staying at. We've now verified this, and that house does belong to a George and Anna Green. We have not yet been able to locate them and are currently in the process of contacting their close relatives in order to gather more information on what might have happened to them. Given the circumstances, we have officially opened up a missing persons case on them."

"*Missing persons*? He killed them, he told me himself. And Anna's diary makes it clear enough what happened."

"Yes, I've seen the diary. But If I may point out, it was you that was living in *their* house."

"But—"

The detective raised his hand again to stop James from making another outburst. "Okay, so the two of you lived there together for a few days... and then things get quite interesting. *You* say here, and I'm paraphrasing, that Elena now tells you of this vast conspiracy involving Cole Bontone getting her to bring you back up to him, so... that he could presumably kill you. Is that about right?" Detective Smith leaned back in his chair. "Now you have to admit, it all sounds a little far-fetched, doesn't it?"

Listening to the detective, James couldn't help but see his point. Even when he initially gave his story to the first detective, he was aware of the *unusual* quality of the events that transpired. Despite his state of mind, he had questioned whether he should alter his narrative into a more believable story or not, but he trusted that the facts and evidence would bring forth the truth of his story in the end. And ultimately, he was not a good liar. Right now, he was again questioning his decision to tell the whole truth, regardless of his innocence. He thought back to that prior morning, when he had first parked on the side of the road in front of the main entrance while it was still dark outside, waiting until they finally opened. The look on the young police officer's face—who James finally got to come out with him—when he looked at the body of Elena lying in the back seat, pale and motionless, her clothing covered in blood. His complexion going white as he stared into the car with his mouth hanging open.

"I know it sounds crazy... but that's how it happened," James said, the pitch and volume in his voice rising. "Did you go up there? Was he there? If you talked to him—if you searched his house—I'm sure there would be some kind of evidence. She wasn't his only victim."

"You say the two of you went up to his house on your own to confront him." Detective Smith paused. "So, what were you planning to do to him? Kill him? If you would've come to us in the beginning—but yes, I know, you had gone over why that wasn't an option." He cleared his throat before continuing, "Anyhow, you say that he thwarted your plan, and after subduing you, he forced the two of you to make a choice. That if one of you killed yourself, the other would be free to go. Am I right?"

"Well... look, I know how it sounds... but yes, that's essentially what happened."

"Then Elena kills herself so you can go free. That is when you come to us."

"Did you talk to Cole or not?" James couldn't keep the hostility out of his voice, tired of listening to the detective evade his questions. His right leg swayed side to side while his hands picked at the Styrofoam cup he was holding.

"James, we have a dead woman—even if it is only a suicide—and a missing couple right near where Cole lives. Beyond this, we now have your story of what happened, which we do take seriously. My partner and I went up to his house yesterday. Cole was there, he even admitted to knowing Elena. He said that he had been seeing her for several weeks until they broke up, which he stated had been about two weeks ago. According to him, she had been severely depressed, and he was worried about her. He fell apart when we informed him of her death, blaming himself for not doing more to help her when he knew the precarious mental state she was in."

The detective stared at James in silence for a moment and then continued, "Naturally, he denied your story completely, and also claims that he doesn't know who you are. We didn't have enough evidence to go to a judge for a search warrant based on your statement alone, but Cole did consent to let us inside his house, as long as we didn't go searching through all the different rooms. As far as Mr. and Mrs. Green go, Cole said that he had only briefly met them once and wasn't aware they were missing."

James sank back into his seat, lowering his head, aware that he wasn't going to get the answers he was looking for.

Detective Smith leaned forward toward James, and went on, "Now, I know you don't want to hear this, but I'm going to tell it to you straight. We don't have any physical evidence right now on Cole Bontone that ties him to Elena's death, or to the disappearance of George and Anna, or to anyone else. And with you being the only witness, it doesn't make things cut and dry. We're still waiting for some tests from Elena's autopsy to come back, but I don't expect to have anything returned that will connect to Cole. The coroner has officially ruled her death a suicide, and whilst slashing one's own throat is an unusual way to go, you yourself say that she committed the physical act herself. As far as Cole indirectly forcing her hand, we can't arrest him on your word alone."

James forced himself to look at the detective waiting for him to finish, continuing to pick away at the cup in his hands, the little Styrofoam pieces laying on the ground by his feet

"Concerning Anna's diary," Smith continued, "it's mostly filled with tormented dreams and feelings, which she then tried to connect to reality. Based on what she wrote, she seemed troubled and probably needed more help than what George could give her. We are looking into people that may have known the Green's and trying to find out what happened to them. Again, all we have is your word that Cole had killed them, and the fact that you were the one staying at their house during this time makes you as much of a suspect in their disappearance as he is. We will continue to investigate this situation and keep an eye on Cole Bontone. With his proximity to the Greene's as well as his own acknowledged relationship with Elena, and then with your allegations regarding what he did, he is definitely a person of interest at the very least, but we cannot arrest him at this point. I'm sorry."

"But he's lying! You have to believe me. Elena didn't just kill herself."

"I can point out that there is an alternative theory to what is happening here. That perhaps you had been in a relationship with Elena, and then she left you for Cole. And when she killed herself, you blamed him. You blamed him to such a degree that you created an elaborate story to say that he killed her."

"But that's ridiculous," James said as he shot up from his chair, leaning his hands against the desk in front of him. "You can't tell me you actually believe that?"

"It's less ridiculous than the story you're giving us," the detective shot James an icy glare that made him sit back down. "Regardless, we have to look at it from all angles. I know this isn't what you wanted to hear, but it isn't over. As we continue to investigate this case, eventually we'll uncover the facts relating to what happened, and if it's as you say that Cole is behind it all, we will get him and bring him in. These things take time, though."

"Okay, I guess there's nothing else I can say. Can I leave now?"

"Yes, of course. But before you do, I want to make myself explicitly clear that you stay away from Cole Bontone. Stay as far away from him as you can. Now is not the time for vigilantism, the law will do its job here. I'll keep in touch with any fresh developments."

James felt his anger seething within as he walked out of the police department. He slammed his car door shut after getting in, then pounded his fist against the dashboard several times. How was he supposed to let it all go, with Cole remaining up on that hill unscathed through it all? And now that Cole knew James had gone to the police, what would he do?

It was late morning as James drove away from the police station. The highway system in Alaska differed from the rest of the United States in that there were very few roads which cut across the vast state. Anchorage bordered along the Cook Inlet in south-central Alaska, and there were only two roads that lead out of the city. There was the Glenn Highway which initially went north-east, before eventually turning more south-east and going into Canada. The other option was the Seward Highway, which lead south into the Kenai Peninsula, and back to where Cole lives.

James knew what he wanted to do at that moment, but he was in no condition to be making that kind of decision right now, not with how hot-headed he was. He drove a few miles south-west to the Far North Bicentennial Park and walked along on some trails there. He talked the situation over with himself for a while until he got sick of hearing his own voice. Then he put on some earbuds and listened to music.

He returned to his car a few hours later, feeling refreshed and clear headed. The hike had sobered him up—even if still a little hung-over—for the first time since getting back into Anchorage, but he was now even more unsure of what to do.

Time passed, and it was late afternoon, fast approaching evening. Not knowing what else to do, James drove several miles south of the city along the Seward Highway. Here the road ran between a stretch of water which was a branch of the Cook Inlet called the Turnagain Arm on one side, and the abrupt rise of a mountain range on the other. He stopped at a deserted pull-off along the road, where there was a rocky shoreline, as opposed to the mud flats which bordered along much of the inlet. After walking along this shoreline for some time, a deepening sense of anguish and anger was building up within James again. He looked out over the inlet, at the mountains still topped with snow bordering the shoreline, but found no calming effect in their beauty. Gazing out over the water, James let out a scream, the sound carrying out across the inlet before finally fading away in the distance. Standing there, he silently called out for guidance, for some form of direction, yet knew that he would receive none.

When James was back in his car, he opened the glove box and grabbed his new handgun. He briefly recalled how on that dark night, just after Elena died, he had dropped his previous gun over a cliff and lost it. Then, yesterday, while he was waiting to hear back from the detective, he visited a gun store and bought a cheap 9mm semi-automatic handgun and a box of ammunition. He didn't know if he would need it or not and had no actual plans of doing anything with it. Placing the gun back in the glove box, he gazed past his dashboard and across the water. He knew he had two options. One was to drive back up past Anchorage and along the Glenn Highway, which would turn east and lead into Canada, where he could then make his way south through Canada and back into the lower forty-eight of the United States. The other option was to continue south along the Seward Highway he was currently on, and drive to where Cole lived. James turned the key, put the car into drive and pulled it to the edge of the highway. Pausing for a moment, he turned the steering wheel and got back onto the road.

CHAPTER 2

James could hardly believe that he was really doing it, that he was really going back to confront Cole again. His stomach was twisting into knots and he couldn't stop his hands from shaking with nervous anticipation of what he was about to do. He couldn't focus on anything for most of his drive down, barely even noticing the mountains and phenomenal views along the road, but as he finally turned off the highway and began driving along a gravel back road, he got a strange sense of déjà vu where everything suddenly became very familiar. He slowed the car almost to a crawl and continued to inch his way along. And then—there. There it was! An unmarked trail heading up the forested slope on the right side of the road. His mind flashed back to when he and Elena had traversed up that trail only several nights ago. The nervous anticipation of what would meet them at the top of the hill as they hiked up the dark path illuminated by their flashlights. The worried expression on Elena's face when she seemed to have some premonition of never coming back down from that hill.

He drove a little further before stopping again. Off to the left was a narrow driveway that he knew very well, though now there was yellow police tape across the entrance. He pictured the house that sat along the edge of the bay at the end of that driveway, which he had stayed at for those several fateful days, feeling a strange urge to walk down that driveway again and see it one last time. James thought back to when Elena asked him if he could really go through with killing Cole. After everything Elena had said that he did, after reading Anna's diary about how he had allegedly harmed other women, he really thought he could, that it was the only option to put an end to the dilemma Cole had put them in. But it was one thing to say it, and another thing altogether in going through with the actual act. He remembered sitting at the kitchen table with Elena as they drew out a map with the trail that led up to his house, discussing their plan of action. They were going to walk to his property from that trail, then run across the open yard toward the back of the house, where they would break in. They would catch Cole off guard and do what needed to be done. It all seemed so simple on paper, but Cole had been two steps ahead of them the whole time and had seen them coming before they had even exited the woods. James shook these thoughts out of his mind and continued driving further down the road, trying to focus on the reason why he had come back here.

He saw what he was looking for, only about a half mile further along the road. Another driveway, this one off to the right, heading up the hill. James followed the drive as it wound its way up the steep slope with a few cutbacks before coming to an end at a garage. James parked the car in front of the closed garage door, not being able to tell if Cole was home or not. After some consideration, he decided to leave his car where it was, knowing that it would be difficult to conceal his presence without parking off the road somewhere and walking all the way up the hill like he had done last time. No, this time he just wanted to get the confrontation done and settled, whatever the consequences may be.

The house didn't seem as dark and ominous in the waning sunshine of this warm day in early May. Yes, the wooden siding was a dark brown and a little weathered, but it appeared like any other normal house. He made his way to the back door, his handgun gripped in his right hand at the ready. He tried the door and, finding it unlocked, cautiously entered the house.

James gripped his handgun in both hands aiming in front of him as he walked into the open living room where he had first woken up tied to a chair on that prior night. Now bathed in the waning sunlight from the large windows, it had a remarkably ordinary and insignificant appearance with its bookshelves and coffee table surrounded by chairs and a sofa. His heart beat rapidly and he tried to still the shakiness in his hands as he moved to the dining room and kitchen. Everything was still, and other than the faint chattering of birds outside, there was only silence. Once he walked through all the rooms upstairs, he was satisfied that Cole was not at home, and resigned himself to waiting for his return. He turned the large recliner in the living room so that it faced the front door and then sat down. He waited, watching the shadows in the room lengthen and the sky outside slowly darken as the sun set.

James woke up with a start, his hand instinctively clenching around the grip of the gun, making sure it was still there. He had fallen asleep. How could he have fallen asleep? He noticed the lights in the room were on and racked his brain trying to remember if he had turned them on himself. A sound like dishes clattering together made James jump out of his seat with a start. He spun around, pointing his gun toward the dining room where he thought he heard the sound. The large rectangular wooden table stood there ominously with its dark stain, which made it appear almost black. Flashes momentarily spun through his head of sitting at that table, Elena across from him, and an elaborate display of food set on the table before them. A sound of glasses clinking forced him back into the present. Someone else was in the house. He heard movement coming from the kitchen. How could he have fallen asleep at a moment like this? He remembered now how he had sat and waited. He waited, and waited, but Cole never showed up, and... and now someone else was here. James moved forward slowly; his legs feeling rigid, his heart rate accelerating rapidly. He approached the dining area and rounded the entryway to the kitchen.

There, standing behind the counter, was none other than Cole Bontone, pouring scotch into a glass. He looked up as he set the bottle back on the counter and locked onto James's gaze.

"'Bout time you've woken up, Jamesy boy. Come and have a drink with me." Cole poured another glass and pushed it across the counter. "And lower that gun, will you? There'll be plenty of time to shoot me after you have a drink."

Hundreds of scenarios on how this moment would unfold had played through James's head over the last few days, but it never started out anything like this. He quickly dropped the magazine out of the gun, and seeing that it was still fully loaded, he slammed it back in and racked the slide, sending the bullet that was already chambered flying to the ground.

Cole laughed awkwardly and then sipped at his drink. "Yes, yes, now come on, we have some catching up to do."

James moved to the counter and stood there for a long moment with the gun still pointed at Cole. His hair was disheveled and greasy as it lay roughly about his brow. Cole had what appeared to be several days length of stubble on his face. He was wearing dark blue jeans and a somewhat wrinkly white button-down shirt with sleeves partly rolled up, and the top two buttons undone. There was a slight slurring of his speech and unsteadiness in his movements. The man in front of him seemed entirely different from the suave, calm and collected Cole Bontone he had seen before.

Cole stared back as he spun his glass on the counter. A smile came across his face, "James Torbour in the flesh, I really wasn't sure if you were ever going to show up again, and after you went to the police... but I'm truly glad to see you, you have no idea. Now drink, then we'll talk some."

James rested the gun on the counter while still holding onto it with his right hand, and with his left, he took the glass of scotch and downed its entire contents, slamming it back on the counter, wincing slightly from the burn.

Cole filled the glass again, then moved around the counter toward James.

James raised the gun again, aiming it at Cole as he continued to slowly walk up to him. Cole stopped with the barrel of the gun mere inches away from his forehead. Then he continued walking around James and to the sliding glass door that led to a patio. "Follow," he said as he walked outside.

James, who had been following Cole's movement with the iron sights of his handgun, walked through the sliding door after him. Cole was sitting in a cloth fold out chair, there was another chair next to him. James slowly moved towards him, sliding the chair a little further away from him before taking a seat.

It was dark, with only the light from inside the house filtering out of the patio doors, and the faint starlight above them. Cole was silent as he grabbed a cigar out of his jacket pocket, offering one to James, who refused with a gesture of his hand. Whilst there wasn't enough light to make out his facial expression, James could see that as Cole lit his cigar with a lighter, his hand was trembling, and he noticed a quiver in his lips. Hearing the faint sound of sniffling, James wondered whether Cole was actually crying.

"I... I don't understand?" James stuttered.

"You know, I knew there was a reason I couldn't do it earlier today," Cole said after a moment of silence. "I had it all ready, all planned out. I went into Seward, took my boat out into the water, past the bay, past the rocky cliffs, and out into the open sea where I was alone with the rolling waves. I thought I was ready, and even started to pour the gasoline... but I couldn't, I... I just fell on my face and wept. Then I sat at the edge of my boat and just drank and smoked until the sun set, at which time I made my way back to the dock and drove back up here."

James heard the unsteadiness of his speech, the words that seemed to be filled with genuine emotion, yet found himself unable to believe what he was hearing.

"When I saw the car in the drive I thought, *now, I could swear that's James's car but...* and then I saw you, sitting in that chair asleep. I think I somehow knew you would end up coming back here again. There is something between us that remains unsettled. Yes, I see it now. This is the way it's supposed to be. That's why I couldn't do it earlier... closure. You Jamesy, you're my closure. You know me better than anyone else, what I've really done."

James wanted to say more, yet he knew he had to be careful in his choice of words. He struggled in his mind for the correct thing to say, but only came up with, "You... seem different."

"I can't get her out of my head. Do you have that same problem? Do you suppose she knew that she was changing everything by what she did? She must have. I mean, Elena was so certain of what she was doing. Was she aware of how utterly she defeated me?

But then, it was really Anna who started it all, the beginning of what would become my final demise. She was the one who made me start to question everything I thought I knew. To wonder if there really is more than just this passing existence. Anna could see right through me, could see exactly who I was... who I am. She was the only person who had ever truly stood up to me before, and she almost succeeded. Then again, I suppose she did win in a way. She never ceases to leave my mind. I am haunted by them both, by their determination, their certainty of why and what they were doing." Cole suddenly got up, dropping his cigar butt to the ground, and walked into the house.

James followed back inside, trying to wrap his head around what Cole was saying and wondering if his visible distress was genuine or if instead this could all be just another twisted game of some sort. In the full artificial lighting of the overhead kitchen lights, James saw Cole unsteadily pour himself another drink and gulp it down eagerly, and James was unsure of what to do, what to feel, or what even to think. It was difficult to feel the same hatred toward him, the same need for revenge that had been consuming James these last few days. But he couldn't forget who this seemingly pitiable man was, what he did, and why James had come back to this horrid place.

Cole was staring at James. Suddenly, he was walking toward him. He aimed the gun at him as he approached. Cole walked up, moving both of his hands to grip the barrel and press it tightly against his forehead. "Well, go ahead and do it then, James, but ask yourself if it's not better to let fate run its course. Killing someone is not an easy burden to carry, and not one that I would now force upon you."

James gripped the firearm with a renewed intensity that made his knuckles start to turn white. All he had to do was pull the trigger and it would be over, but this wasn't the way it was supposed to happen. It all felt wrong now. How could he kill Cole like this, when none of it felt justified any longer? Sweat was dripping down his forehead as he stood there in indecision.

With both hands wrapped around the barrel, Cole lowered the gun away from his head. "Now—now, let it go. Let it go, James, let all the emotions just pass right through you." With the gun pointed toward the ground, Cole let go of his grip.

James stared back at Cole, inwardly searching for some kind of decisive action to take, but disoriented by Cole's unexpected actions, he did nothing.

Cole stepped forward and wrapped his arms around James in a tight embrace. Whispering in his ear, Cole said, "I'm scared, James. More than I have ever been in my entire life. I'm sorry, I know that doesn't matter now, but I am." Then he released James and made his way past the dining area, and through to the living room, before starting up the stairs.

James took a brief moment to collect himself before following Cole up the stairs. Reaching the top, he looked across the corridor of rooms and saw light spilling out of one of them. The scent of gasoline fumes hit him before he even got to the open doorway. Peering inside, he saw Cole sitting on a bed with his back toward him. James could see him holding up a necklace. It had a thin gold chain with a green stone of some sort. Cole looked at it for a moment before dropping it out of sight behind the bed. He then brought some article of clothing up to his face before letting it slip through his fingers onto the bed.

"It all means nothing... every, single, one." Cole turned his head and looked back at James. "You know what scares me more than anything else? It's the possibility that this life we live right now isn't the only existence, as I've always believed." He took a lighter out of his pocket and flicked the flint a few times to watch the flame appear and disappear on and off. "What if there's more than this? I think it's long overdue that I find out. I've seen far too much death not to have faced my own." Cole lit the lighter again, this time bringing some clothing—a red dress—up to meet the flame. When the flames were licking halfway up the garment, Cole dropped it into a box that held various other women's clothing and items, watching as they all instantly ignited into flame. He stood up and faced James. "It's time for you to leave now. There is only fire and death here." He moved to the side of the room and grabbed a shotgun. The bed had now caught fire, and the flames were rapidly spreading and filling the room with smoke. Cole racked the slide and sat on the edge of the bed that wasn't yet on fire. He placed the end of the barrel underneath his chin with the butt of the gun braced against the ground. He strained his right arm down so that he barely reached the trigger with his finger. His eyes flicked at James, who was still standing in the doorway. "Why are you still here?" Cole said, coughing from the smoke surrounding him. "Run, you fool. Forget about me."

James tucked the gun he was still holding into his waistband and stumbled back against the wall, turning toward the stairs. He staggered downward, bracing his hand against the wall for balance as he went, taking in short, shaky breaths.

A boom echoed down the hallway, and James fell against the railing at the top of the stairs as he heard the discharge of the shotgun from the room. He looked back and saw the flickering light of the flames that were consuming the room, and the billowing smoke pouring out. Floundering down the stairs, he barely managed to not completely fall over. He ran to the door he had first entered, continuing to rush down the path to his car.

James stood against the driver's side door of his car and looked up at the house. Flames were now licking up the outside of the second-story bedroom window and began to spread across the siding. He stood and watched, unable to move or do anything else. His eyes latched onto the bright flames as they spread and consumed the rest of the house, and he watched as the entire side of the house became engulfed in fire and smoke before getting into the car. As he pulled away, he could see the pillar of black smoke pouring into the sky in his rearview mirror.

CHAPTER 3

James took another tug from the bottle of whiskey and a moment later finished the energy drink, tossing the can on the floor with the other empty he had finished earlier. The speedometer reminded him to keep his speed down, reducing his chances of being pulled over or veering off the road. He was thankful that the highway was empty at this late hour. The adrenaline that still hadn't subsided was keeping him focused on his driving, despite how much he'd had to drink. Knowing that the border was still a long way away, he still wanted to put as many miles on the road as he could to close that distance.

James could not recollect when he had left Cole's burning house, or how long he had been driving for as he continued to stare into the darkness beyond the narrow beam of his headlights, hands clenched to the steering wheel and still driving too fast as *Rammstein* blared through the speakers. He eased up on his grip and tried to relax as he thought about how he was now far north of Anchorage, finding some happiness in knowing that he would probably never see it again. His eyes were heavy now, and as his vision blurred, he knew he had to stop soon. Looking at the dashboard clock that read 4:30, he parked at the next pullout along the road. He closed his eyes and let himself drift off to sleep.

The sound of faint voices stirred him awake, and he shifted in his seat, feeling the stiffness in his back. He saw a young couple outside taking some pictures, then get back into their car and continue driving down the road. James glanced at the clock, which now read 11:53. He stepped out of his car and looked at the view surrounding him. Before him was a sloping hill covered with tall and narrow spruce trees descending into a wide river basin with snow-topped mountains rising on the opposite side. When he was back on the road, he silently admonished himself for sleeping so long. He had looked at where he was on a map and estimated that he still had an almost six-hour drive to the border, which meant he could still probably make it across that day if he just drove.

His mind drifted back to Cole and what had happened. It was now finished, over, so why did James still feel so empty? Elena was still dead, leaving him to pick up the pieces, to fulfill a promise in making his life matter. Tears came to his eyes as he remembered her, the wind tossing her long blonde hair, the rare smile, the spark in her eyes when she looked at him. The light of the several fires scattered about the lawn casting an inconsistent light upon her pleading face as she held that knife in her shaky hand, saying, "This is where my story ends, but yours doesn't have to. It can't. It's up to you, James, to do the right thing. Move on, but don't forget about me."

To do the right thing, her words echoed in his head. But how was he supposed to do that, to know what the right thing even was? Cole was dead, but he knew that wasn't what she was referring to. The dark shadow in James's mind was still there, the empty pit within himself hadn't closed. Would he have felt better if he had pulled the trigger himself, if he had fulfilled his vengeance with his own hand? No, but now he had to find a way to move on, and getting out of the state was the first step.

Detective Smith then came to mind. If James had been a prime person of interest regarding Elena's death, how even more so now in Cole's? Smith would undoubtedly go after him now, especially once he crossed the border into Canada, which didn't exactly make him look innocent. He pushed all of that aside. He couldn't stay here, he had to get away, and he knew Smith would never believe what happened if James told him. No, he would worry about that later. Right now he had the road which stretched out endlessly before him with all the possibilities that it held.

In the town of Tok, James stopped for a burger at a restaurant and then continued driving. It was mid-afternoon now, and the pressing desire he had earlier to cross the border that day had left him. Now he just wanted to find a place to camp and rest after being in the car for so long. Making note of the mile markers he passed, he pulled off into one of the many scenic overlooks along the road, taking little heed of the vista with a mountain range stretching across the landscape off in the distance. He pulled out the *Milepost*, a road guide he had used when he had first travelled into the state, which listed virtually everything there was to know along the main highways in Alaska, along with the major routes into the state from Canada. The book listed everything from road conditions to gas stations and campsites. He found Deadman Lake Campground listed as being only another few miles up the road.

James drove through the campground nestled in a spruce dominated forest, seeing that only a few of the fifteen total sites were occupied. He chose a campsite surrounded by trees near the adjacent lake the campground was named for. It was a warm and sunny day, and James could look through a few trees and see the lake from his site. He set up his tent and got settled, and then made a fire, heating a can of soup for his supper. Several grouse walked by as he ate, and when he finished, James made his way along a trail, following the edge of the lake. After taking a seat on a log, he looked at a line of snow-topped mountains far in the distance along the horizon. He listened to music as ducks lazily swam by while the sun lowered in the West. The stiffness in his joints from driving for so long had started to fade and he could feel his stress easing away. The scenery and wildlife surrounding him, along with the clean fresh air, seemed to push the events of the last several days to the back of his mind. He was able to close his eyes and let the music wash over him, quieting his mind. He went back to his campsite and sat next to the fire until after it got dark, then he got into the tent, falling asleep soon after he slipped into his sleeping bag.

The next morning, he noticed he had a missed call with a voicemail. He listened to it, hearing a familiar voice through the speaker. "Hi James, this is detective Smith. I'm calling to inform you about some news regarding the case on Elena. Cole is dead. There was a fire and his house burned down. We discovered his body amongst the wreckage. Look James, I'm going to need you to come back in. There are a few more questions I have to ask you. Call me back." Smith's voice was flat and with little inflection.

It was a call James had expected, but it still came as a bit of a shock to listen to the actual message, and for a moment made him question what he was doing. Anchorage was many miles behind him now and he was now only about an hour away from crossing the border. As he thought about his options, his course of action remained clear. He would continue into Canada and drive down into the lower forty-eight. Driving back to Anchorage wasn't an option, not after he was already this far, and he couldn't bear the thought of sitting across from Smith again, listening to him all but accuse him of killing Cole. He knew this was something that he couldn't just run away from, but surely it could wait until he was through Canada and in the state of Washington, where he would have some time and distance from everything that happened. Then he could tell them everything they needed to know, but not now. Right now, he just couldn't deal with all of that.

Back on the road, unease and a sense of foreboding were upon him again. He mentally went over the voicemail the detective left him, which then led to thoughts about Cole and Elena as well. James hoped that once he crossed the border, he would be able to relax a little, as if the physical act of leaving Alaska and entering another country would also somehow correspond to a mental and emotional distancing from the events which occurred there as well. As he continued driving, he remembered his handgun. Canada didn't allow handguns into the country and although he could try to smuggle it across, there was the chance that they would search his car and find it. As he thought about this, he realized he didn't even want to carry it anymore and would be almost relieved to be rid of it. When the road came along a wide river, he saw a place to pull over and got out. He walked down a gentle slope through a line of spruce trees, which soon gave way to willows and alder along the bank of the river. Stepping onto the pebbles along the water's edge and looking around to be sure he was alone, he pulled out his 9mm handgun, looking at it. He dropped the mag and racked the slide, verifying it was unloaded. Then he disassembled it and threw the separate parts into different areas of the river.

When he saw the Canadian border checkpoint ahead, his hands suddenly became sweaty, and his mouth was dry to where he even had trouble swallowing. Erratic questions flashed through his head. *Did detective Smith notify them to stop him if he tried to cross the border? Could he have already issued an arrest warrant and they'll put me in cuffs the moment they run my name?* He hoped these rambling thoughts were completely irrational, but he didn't know how these things worked.

When he handed his passport to the officer, his hands moved in abrupt and jerky motions, and he was jumpy when asked the standard questions, "What's your reason for visiting Canada? How long do you plan to stay? Have you ever been convicted of a serious crime? Do you have any firearms with you?"

James stumbled and stuttered through his answers, "Travelling... to—into Washington state. A few days, maybe four or five. No. N—no." He knew that his nervousness must be clear to the officer, which only made his actions even more unnatural. He was sure they were going to wave him off to the side to answer more questions or search his vehicle, but then the officer was handing him back his passport and saying, "Thank you for visiting Canada. Have a nice day."

Just like that, he was on his was on his way again. The road was rough, filled with potholes and broken pavement from frost heaves, but he was out of Alaska and into the land of Tim Hortons and gas stations where you didn't pump your own gas. The sight of a 90 km/h sign strangely comforted him as it signaled the fact that he was somewhere foreign and thus distant from where he had been, even though the scenery was generally the same as before with spruce dominated forests and snowy mountain ranges. He saw a black bear taking a few steps along the opposite lane of the road ahead of him. The bear stopped and stared at James as he slowly drove by.

An audiobook played through the car stereo and James eased back into his seat, letting the vast open landscape of spruce forests spotted with lakes and bogs that gave rise to the distant mountains combine with the narration of the book and fill his mind. The shadowy thoughts relating to Cole, Elena, and the investigation gave way and for a little while withdraw into the recesses of his thought. *This is good,* he thought, *hundreds, even thousands of miles of open road, where I can just drive.* He let himself relax as much as he was able, to empty his head and fill it with only the road directly ahead of him. The weight of the debt Elena left him with when she died was something James was always conscious of. The responsibility of making his life matter now, of doing the right thing, of not letting her death mean nothing. But the prospect of how to fulfill such an obligation was still overwhelming to him. So instead, he thought about the several days of driving through Yukon and British Columbia that were now ahead of him as he headed toward Washington. What he did after that was something he would figure out when that time came.

CHAPTER 4

Whitehorse was the largest city in Yukon, Canada, even with a population under 30,000. James checked into a hotel right in town and near the Yukon River, which ran along the city. The floorboards creaked beneath the stained carpeting and there was low water pressure, but it was a definite step up from camping. James took a shower, changed into clean clothes, and then walked to the river. It was mid-afternoon when James started walking on the paved path which followed beside the river, bordered by mown grass and the occasional manicured tree. The path was situated with the river running along on the East side, and the city to the West, where various renovated historic buildings sat alongside of it.

He had walked by many people, both old and young, who were also out enjoying this warm day in May, and after continuing for some time, he was now moving out of the city. He was about to turn back as he passed a small group of people standing next to a tree just off the path. One of them caught James's eye as he was walking past.

"Hey, how's it going?"

"Oh, pretty good," James said, pausing in his stride and looking at the man who had addressed him. He had a somewhat darker complexion with a native look to him and dark hair that fell just past his shoulders, late twenties, if James had to guess his age.

"Not a bad evening out, not at all. We're just doing a little drinking out here." The man gestured with his hand that was holding a bottle covered by a brown paper bag.

"Yeah, that's cool."

"You want some?"

"Nah…" but as James was saying it, he changed his mind. What the hell, after all. "Well, sure actually, if you're offering."

The man handed James the bottle, and he took a small swig and then handed it back to him.

"I'm Ray," the man said as he held his empty hand out.

"James, nice to meet you," he said, shaking his hand.

"Where you from, James?"

"Well, I'm originally from Illinois, but I'm coming back down from Alaska. Headed back to the lower forty-eight."

"Illinois? Alaska? Hey Marcos, check it out, this guy's American."

"Hey, you guys have paper money over there, right?" Marcos asked, moving next to Ray. He appeared to be

Hispanic with closely buzzed hair which was shaved on the sides.

"Yeah, that's right, it's paper."

"Can I see it? I've never seen American money before, ours is all plastic. Are you guys going to use plastic money soon, too?"

"I don't know, not that I know of." James pulled a dollar bill out of his wallet. "Here you go, one dollar."

"Cool." Ray snapped the bill from James's hand, "Marcos, one American dollar, here you go. This is worth like, a lot where you're from, right?"

Marcos laughed, "Yeah, I'll take this back to Mexico, and I'll like, be so rich, you know."

An older man that was with them who turned out to be Ray's father began talking to James, explaining that his other son, Ray's brother, had just been convicted the day before on some drug possession charge, and so now a few of his friends and family had come out here to do some drinking and reminiscing. The man then talked about the city of Whitehorse and how it had changed so much since he was a kid. "All of this back here used to be woods," he was saying, "Now it's all fast food and chain stores, concrete and subdivisions. This city used to be different, but this is the way things go. What are you gonna do?"

James nodded in agreement, but thought the whole situation was rather strange, and wondered why they had stopped him and taken such an interest in talking to a stranger such as himself. Did they immediately single him out as being an American and found some kind of fascination with that? None of it made sense.

"Hey, so James," Ray said, getting his attention, "we're going to be hanging out at some bars a little later tonight. Why don't you come and join us? It's gonna be a *night*, you know."

James hesitated in responding, thinking of how to decline the invitation politely. He wasn't in the mood to go partying with some random strangers.

"What's your phone number? I'll text you the time and place and you can meet us there," Ray said before James managed a reply.

"I don't know if I'm going to make it out there tonight. I—"

"Nonsense," Ray said, interrupting James, "it'll be fun. You'll just be sitting in a hotel room, otherwise, am I wrong?"

"Well... I suppose." James was about to give him a fake number, but then changed his mind at the last moment, giving out the real one instead, as a small part of him thought he might take him up on that offer after all.

"Great, I'll see you a little later then."

James tried to make sense of what had just happened as he walked back toward the hotel. Why did they single him out to talk to him? Why did they invite him to the bars with them? He tried to shake away the uneasiness he felt, telling himself it was just one of those random encounters you have, but it remained there, lingering in his thoughts.

Once he got back into his hotel room, he put headphones on and went to lie on the bed, listening to music. After a little while, he closed his eyes and let his mind wander. Drifting back to when he was standing on the Alaskan shoreline during one of the early days after he discovered the beautiful vacant house near Seward before he had ever met Elena. A smile spread across his face as he gazed at the mountains across the bay, when everything he was looking at was still new to him. He remembered a very specific moment, where he was listening to music and smoking a cigar, with a half empty bottle of wine in the sand next to him. The combining factors of the buzz, music, and place he was in at that moment made him feel as if he could do anything he wanted. Nothing was impossible if he just set his mind to it. That felt like so long ago now, even though in actuality, it was only a few weeks.

James's phone vibrated, interrupting his thoughts. It was a text message that read, *this is Ray. We're on our way to a bar called The Saloon. Meet us there as soon as you can.*

It was an odd thing, because despite the strange way in which he had met Ray and Marcos, and knowing nothing about them, he found himself inclined to meet them now. He wasn't sure what brought on this change from earlier, whether he simply wanted to spend a night surrounded by people instead of by himself again, or if there was something more to it than that, but James found himself now resolved to go. He looked up the location on his phone, then threw on a different shirt, slid his shoes on, and after briefly running his hands through his hair, he was on his way.

The Saloon wasn't that far from his hotel, so he walked. The sun was going down, and he passed by the occasional hotel, diner, and various other businesses before reaching his destination several blocks away. *The Saloon's* front was of a natural wood siding, giving it a bit of a rustic feel, but the thing that really caught the eye were the two life-size moose carvings standing on the overhanging roof in a pose with their antlers clashing together. Standing in front of the doorway, he hesitated, feeling a vague sense of foreboding as a shadow passed over his mind. He shrugged the feeling off, telling himself it was just anxiety, and passed inside.

James looked around for Ray and the others, not seeing them. It was larger inside than he expected, with a long bar running along the right side with a wall of liquor bottles behind it, and to the left, there were various tables. Further back there were two pool tables which were currently covered up, and then along the back wall there was a mess of speakers and cords where a woman appeared to be setting up for a gig, and was doing some sound checks. James squeezed his way through the crowd as he went up to the butcher block bar top, where he ordered a gin and tonic from an attractive middle-aged woman. He scanned the room again, looking for the people he was supposed to be meeting, but didn't see anyone he recognized. Moving away from the press of people and chatter that surrounded the bar, James went and sat down at an empty table off to the side where he could watch for Ray a little better.

What am I even doing here? Why am I doing any of this? I'll just finish this drink and get out of here, and that'll be that. Who knows If Ray and them are actually even coming. James was staring at his glass of gin and tonic, not paying any attention to the woman who was introducing herself onstage. A slow melody on a guitar was being played while James remained staring at the cloudy drink on the table. When the woman began singing, James finally looked up, realizing that this band only comprised the one woman. The music had an Indie folk vibe with a subdued and ambient quality to it. Her singing had this sadness and emotional rawness to it which, when combined with the music she was playing, had this beauty which resonated strongly with James. The sound seeming to envelope itself around him like a comforting shroud, as if telling him it was okay to feel what he was feeling, that within sadness and even melancholia itself there can be a beautiful comfort to be found. His attention was immersed in watching and listening to this woman play, the music almost seeming to evoke an uplifting quality in it despite its sadness. Almost without realizing it, James's mind drifted, hearing waves crash upon rock, the smell of the salt sea. Walking between the water's edge and a towering cliff, the sight of sea lions sunbathing on exposed rocks at low tide. Gazing into a horizon where the sky blends with the ocean, feeling... contentment.

Being enveloped within the music the way he was, all the ambient noise within the bar—the ceaseless chatter, intermittent laughter and arguments—completely disappeared as far as his perception went. Everyone in the bar seemed to vanish, leaving James with a feeling like it was just him and the woman with the feathery voice and guitar, and no one else in the entire bar. Perhaps it was that dreamy, almost ethereal voice she had, or maybe his current state of mind, but he felt a wave of emotion and a feeling of loss come over him as Elena rose in his mind. For a moment, he put aside his part in what happened that night—his actions, failures, and guilt—took himself completely out of it, and looked at it from a different viewpoint. Elena made her own choice, and perhaps she did it for herself as much as anyone else. He thought back to what Cole said later, about her defeating him in the end. Did she know then what results her action would bring? As horrible as it was, in the end, she had taken control of her own fate. She played Cole's twisted game, and now he was dead, and James was still alive, so perhaps she really did win. But James still couldn't put aside the fact that he owed his life to what she had done, and now had to find a way to live up to such a price.

A tap on the shoulder jolted James out of this state of mind, flinching at the touch, he twisted around in his chair. Abruptly, he heard all the voices of the people in the bar thunder back into his head, surprised to see that the large, open area had become even more crowded now. There was a sizable group of maybe twenty people that had gathered in front of the woman playing music, most of them younger. Two women stood out in front of the others, swaying, and seeming to be caught up in the music as much as he had been.

"Did you hear me?" Ray asked. He had his hair tied back in a ponytail now and was wearing a casual button-down shirt. "We never saw you come in and figured you were flaking out on us when Marcos finally noticed you over here in the corner."

Marcos, the Hispanic who had taken his American one-dollar bill, was standing right beside Ray in a tight-fitting V-neck. James also noticed a woman whom he had seen with them on the walkway but never talked to; and then there were two other people behind them he hadn't met.

Ray noticed his gaze. "I don't think I ever formally introduced you to Tehya, my fiancé." Tehya was of a darker complexion and clearly looked of native descent, with long, straight black hair. "And this is Freddy and his girl, Emily." As Ray gestured toward them, they moved forward and greeted James as well. Freddy fit the hipster look perfectly with his pompadour hairstyle and groomed beard, along with his skinny jeans. Emily was wearing a white beanie which only partially covered her shoulder length platinum blonde hair.

They went over to the bar, with everyone ordering more drinks and chattering amongst themselves. Their conversation revolved around Ray's brother Damien, going over what had happened at court the day before and how he was now going to be serving a short prison sentence. Not having any part in their discussion, James sipped on another gin and tonic. His view of the woman playing the guitar was now obscured, but he focused on the music, withdrawing into his mind once again.

"James. James, what do you think? How about it?"

"What?" James snapped his attention over to Ray, who had been speaking to him. "Sorry, how about what?"

"About going along with us. You're headed down to the states, right? So why not drive with us down to Vancouver, unless you're taking a different route, and even then, we can still travel together until our paths part?"

James stared blankly at Ray for a moment, trying to process what he said. How long had he zoned out of this conversation, and how did it ever get to this pointed question without him even being a part of it? "So, you're driving to Vancouver, all of you?"

"That is what we've been talking about. Damn James, you haven't been drinking that much, have you? Keep up."

"Yeah man," Marcos said, stepping in beside him, "It's gonna be fantastic, my friend, just fantastic.

There's just something about being on the road right. I mean, it won't be the same without Damian, but he had to get in trouble with the law—again—the fool. His absence leaves us one man short, however, and now here *you* are, heading the same way and everything."

"We're all going to the same place, so why not," Tehya added, as she moved closer to him. "You may as well drive with us, the more the merrier and all that."

James's head was spinning with thoughts. Who are these people that they would ask him to travel with them? Why did Ray stop him on the outskirts of town to talk earlier? Why had he been singled out? Why him? He had no idea who these people really were, and they didn't know him either. None of it made sense. Why would they want *him* to tag along with them, a stranger they had just met? On the other hand, if this was all as innocent as they made it sound, perhaps it wouldn't be so bad to have some company while on the road.

"Look James," Ray said, "It wouldn't be much different from if you were still on your own. You would just follow along and camp with us, yet still be able to break away and leave whenever you needed to. With Damian not going, it just feels like we're one man short, I guess, and somehow it just seems like you'd be a good fit with our little group. It's totally up to you, but either way, we're leaving tomorrow morning."

There seemed to be some sense in Ray's words. *It wouldn't be much different from being on your own. Still be able to break away whenever you needed to.* There was something pleasing about the prospect of still having all those hours while driving to himself, but yet be part of a group of people he could talk to and hang out with at camp. But even if he could leave them at any point, how could he trust them? How could he just believe everything these people were saying was the truth? No, he couldn't, not after everything that had happened. He needed to be alone, to distance himself and his thoughts from recent events. He couldn't allow himself to get caught up in the complications, drama, and whatever else traveling with this crew might entail.

"I don't know. I'll have to think about it," James said.

"I understand. Sleep on it and you can let us know in the morning." Ray lifted his bottle, and then everyone except James toasted to the next few days when they would be on the road together.

James wished he had been more honest and just declined to travel with them outright instead of making it sound like he was still unsure. He felt there was suddenly no reason to stay there any longer when Marcos ordered a round of shots. He downed his glass, the sting feeling bitter in the back of his throat. "Hey,

I'm sorry, but I have to get going. I'll text you what I decide in the morning."

"Oh, all right," Ray said with a hint of disappointment in his voice, standing up from his stool. "Well, it was great hanging out, and I hope to see you tomorrow. We plan to be leaving around nine or so."

The feel of the cool night air hitting his face as he exited the bar felt refreshing. He was happy to have the whole subject of traveling with Ray behind him now, but the question of why he was even invited in the first place lingered with him. The streets were mostly empty as he walked along the city sidewalk, awash in the yellow glow of the sodium street lamps overhead. Walking through the soft shadows brought an image to his mind of Elena's silhouette in the moonlight as she stood near the water's edge, a pang of loss and guilt passing through him at the memory. He breathed in deeply, feeling the caress of the cool night breeze, and listening to the sound of an occasional passing car.

When he arrived back at his hotel, he spent little time in getting to bed, but he found sleep difficult as his mind remained restless long into the night.

CHAPTER 5

The woods seemed to be encroaching upon him, towering pines and old twisted maples covered in moss all around. A heavy mist hovered beneath the high canopy of green above as a faint breeze seemed to hiss along the forest floor, carrying with it faint indefinable whispers, as if the trees themselves were speaking amongst each other. Fear and foreboding hung upon his mind like the mists surrounding him, and one word seemed to scream out to him: *run!* He couldn't see far in the mist as he ran across the heavy leaf litter and ferns. Something wrapped around his leg, and he fell to the ground. Looking back, he saw a hand gripped onto his ankle. To his growing horror, he saw that the arm was reaching up from beneath the ground. Struggling frantically, he couldn't break free from the hand's iron grip. The sound of breaking earth caused him to glance back again to see another arm come up from the ground, bracing its hand against the mossy forest floor, pushing the rest its body up from the beneath the soil. The leaf strewn ground heaved and began to rise up, followed by loose dirt falling away from a human form.

A terrible yet faintly recognizable face rose up to meet his, and James screamed. Her dirty blonde hair fell raggedly about her face, where small strips and pieces of flesh had started to peel and rot away. Elena gave him a crooked smile, hideous in appearance—a centipede crawling out of the corner of her mouth, scurrying behind her hair. She let go of his leg and awkwardly rose to her to feet, arching her spine and twisting her head to the side, cracking several bones into place before standing upright.

Fear had shocked James into a state of immobility as he sat on the ground, staring up at her. Her clothing hung loosely about her, mud-caked and tattered.

"James... come with me." Her voice was hoarse and cracked, as she now held out her hand for him to take. "The earth is warm, and dark. Rest your bones next to my own. The road you're on will lead you here in the end after all." She took a step, staggering toward him.

"No! No, get away from me." James scrambled up, before stumbling to the ground in his haste.

"No James! Don't leave. Don't leave... me!" Her coarse earthy voice turning to a scream sounding more animal than human,

James ran, glancing back once more to see her stagger forward as a bone in one of her legs seemed to snap, causing her to fall to the ground.

"Don't leave! James!"

"No!" James screamed, sitting bolt upright in the bed. Daylight streamed into the hotel room as the sound of vibrating made him look over and grab his phone, seeing that he had received a text. His heart was racing as he read it, trying to force the image of that screaming face out of his mind.

We're almost set, wheels rolling in 45. I'm sure I'll see you soon.

James dropped the phone on the table and laid back into the bed, taking a few seconds to realize what the text was referring to. Another text followed with an address of where to meet. He couldn't get the dream out of his head. *That face. Why did it have to be her face?* He had been having nightmares ever since she died, but never any like this, polluting his memory of her true face and person. His dreams were supposed to be getting better, not worse, as he travelled further away from what happened. He had believed that the road and the accumulation of miles between him and that place where everything happened would make him feel better. But this didn't seem to be the solution he was looking for. What if nothing changed, if nothing got better? What if, after everything that happened, darkness remained the only thing waiting for him at the end of the long road? Suddenly, the road no longer held the same sense of freedom and escape that it previously held. Something had to change. He had to find another way.

James shot to his feet, looking at the clock. *I can still go with them; I still have time.* With hardly another thought, he was in the bathroom taking a shower. In a rush, he began preparing to leave, brushing his teeth, throwing his clothes into his bag, looking up the address on his phone. He barely let himself think about what he was doing, about why he had suddenly changed his mind to go with them. All he was certain of in that moment was that his current course of action wasn't working, nothing was getting better, so now he was jumping at the one chance he saw to make that decaying face go away, hoping it would never come back.

When he was in his car, he looked at the clock again. *Okay, I still have time.* James closed his eyes and breathed in deeply. He had one last opportunity to change his mind, to just leave, and have nothing but the open road and himself—with dark shadows of the past ever chasing him, and the rotting visage of Elena haunting his dreams. He grabbed his phone.

Leaving now, I'll be there in five.

He pulled into a parking lot of a closed storefront, seeing Ray and Tehya right away, and then noticing the rest of the group as he parked next to the other cars, which evidently belonged to them.

"James! Hey, it's great to see you again," Ray said as James came walking towards him from his car. "Some of us weren't sure if you'd show up. You've actually won me ten bucks, so thanks for that. I won't say who bet against you, though. We'll be ready to roll in a few. You can just sit tight if you're ready—but wait, I have something for you."

James leaned against the car door as Ray grabbed something from his vehicle.

"Here," Ray handed him a radio, "We'll be using these to keep in touch whilst on the road. Just keep it on channel 9."

Getting back in his car, James sat back in his driver's seat, situating the two-way radio in his console. Was he really doing this, about to set off on a road trip with these people he had just met? He thought about how he had been so set in his decision to not travel with them the night before, and now here he was. Because of what, one nightmare? Already it was receding into the back of his mind, losing the horror which had been so pressing upon his mind only an hour ago. Was he crazy? Was he making a big mistake now? He tried to focus on why he made this decision, how being around people must be better than remaining on his own. That's what he hoped, anyway. They all seemed to be normal friendly people, and there wasn't any sign that this would be anything other than what they claimed, as simply being a group of friends taking a road trip together... with him tagging along.

The passenger side door of his car suddenly opened and a woman that he had never seen before began shoving things that were on the passenger seat toward the back of the car.

"Boy, you sure have a lot of crap in this car don't you," the woman said as she was struggling to jam a plastic bag filled with miscellaneous items between the back of her seat and a sleeping bag that was pressing against it. "Stuff—I mean, I don't presume to call what someone else has as crap. You know, one man's crap is another man's... stuff, and so on." She looked at James now, who was staring back at her with a stern expression, the muscles in his face turning hard and rigid. "I'm Sofie, by the way."

"What?" It was the only word he could find to say, although internally he thought, *of course, I should've known better than to take Ray at his word. What have I just gotten myself into?*

"Sofie, I'll be riding with you on the trip down." She looked back at the luggage and belongings that James had stacked to the ceiling in the back seat. "It is a little cramped in here, but that's all right. How *do* you see behind you, though?"

"What I mean to say is, what are you doing in *here*?"

"I believe I just told you. You *are* James, right?"

"Yes, but—"

"Great! I'm excited, aren't you? Look, I can't stop shaking." She held her hand out horizontally in front of her to show the shakiness of it. "Of course, that's probably just the coffee. I think I drank like five cups already."

"The thing is, it seems Ray has neglected to mention that you would ride along with me.

"You're kidding?" Sofie said, and then started laughing. "Ha, that's just like Ray. It doesn't surprise me much at all really, he never was very good in the way of passing along information. Well, the original plan was that Damian, Ray's brother, was going to be taking his rig down, and then I—or Marcos—was going to ride down with him, before he got arrested, of course. Freddy and Emily only have their little coupe with them, why they don't have a larger vehicle living up here in Yukon, Canada, one may never know, and it's probably good that they're going to be staying in Vancouver, as I don't think they're really cut out to live all the way up here. Anyway, this is simply to say that they barely have enough room for their luggage, let alone another passenger. Ray and Tehya's SUV is larger and would normally hold four people no problem, but that thing's filled with so much stuff, including my own luggage, that Marcs is lucky to have a seat himself. Sure, I could probably cram myself back there for all 2,400 kilometers to Vancouver if I absolutely had to, but no thank you, and now with you being with us, I don't have to worry about that. Isn't that great?"

The two-way radio came on, and Ray's voice sounded through the speaker, *"Allllllright—alright—alright, everyone ready to go now? We've got a lot of miles to cover, so stay light on liquids and tighten those seat belts because we're about ready to burn rubber and blow this town yip-yip-yip."*

"Oh yeah, you betcha-ay," came what James guessed was Freddy's voice in what seemed to be some imitation of a stereo-typical Canadian accent, which seemed odd, considering that Freddy appeared to be a Canadian himself from the little that James knew of him.

"Yeah, I guess we're ready," James said through the radio. He was about to point out that Ray never mentioned that Sofie would need to ride along in his car, but then thought better of it. *So much for a peaceful drive all by myself. We haven't even left yet and already the nature of this road trip has changed. What else will change before we reach our destination?* The SUV in front of him jerked forward with a brief squeal of the tires, followed by Freddy's coupe, with James following last in his own sedan.

"Yeah, I might regret all that coffee I drank in another hour, here's hoping my bladder can hold out," Sofie looked at James, and in that same exuberant manner in which she had been talking, continued to say, "Well, we're off on the open road now, mostly just vast forest wilderness and mountains for most of the drive all the way to Vancouver. Isn't it just exhilarating?"

James took a quick moment to look at her. She spoke with a European accent, maybe Swedish or somewhere in that region. Her long dark brown hair, which fell well past her shoulders, framed her narrow face and pale complexion nicely. "I guess so," he replied, looking back at the road, aware of his iron grip upon the steering wheel which was the only outward sign of his anger and frustration, while within he tried to come to grips with the fact that everything he had thought this trip was going to be had now completely changed.

They were driving south out of the city now and back on Highway 1—also known as the Alaska Highway, or the Alaska-Canadian Highway, or ALCAN, depending on who you were to ask. The landscape within their immediate vicinity was flat, with fir and spruce off to either side of the wide shoulders of the road. Off in the distance, they could see mountains rising above the treetops.

"Look, I'm sorry that you weren't expecting me to be here," Sofie said, breaking the short period of silence. "You really didn't know I was going to be riding along with you in your car, huh? It really is a win-win though if you think about it. I'll of course go fifty-fifty on gas, so you'll save money there, and I don't have to be crammed into the back of the SUV next to Marcos, and then finally and I would say this is the most important, you get the pleasure of my company instead of being stuck with just yourself and being bored out of your mind. So, it's actually a double win for you and a win for me, so more like a win-win-win, really."

"A win-win... win, huh? Lucky me." James tried not to sound too sarcastic.

"Just you wait. In a few hours, you're going to wonder how you ever got so lucky as to have me here with you for the drive. You're welcome in advance by the way, we just need some music is all. Do you have anything good—never mind, I have my collection. Do you have a jack for a phone—okay, here we are," Sofie plugged her phone into the car. "So, what do you want to listen to?"

"I don't care."

"Okay, well..." After momentarily searching on her phone, music started playing. Sofie leaned back in the seat with her head tilted up slightly as she closed her eyes. "Team me."

"What?" James asked.

Sofie looked over at him. "The band that's playing, they're called *Team Me*. They're from Norway, just like me."

"Oh. So, you're Norwegian huh,"

"Yes, or did you think my accent was Canadian, eh?"

"No, I knew it was European. I just didn't—"

"I'm messing with you, James."

"Right, so what brings you to Canada? Not to say there's anything wrong with Canada, it's just that when I think of Norway, I think of..."

"Mountains, grand mountains and majestic fjords, the ocean, the aurora borealis lighting up the night sky, people and towns that have true character and a feel that is distinctively Norwegian. So, in a way like Canada, only..."

"Not Canada?" James ventured questioningly.

"Definitely *not* Canada. Norway is home. When I left, I think a piece of myself remained back there on those long distant shores. Sofie's tone took on a hint of sadness as she gazed out at the passing trees. "Canada's fine, you know, I guess... but, well, I don't know. It's not home. I never thought I would miss it so much when I left... ahh well, that's how it goes, I suppose. And I am looking forward to seeing Vancouver again." Sofie pulled a pack of cigarettes out, tapping the bottom of the box against her palm a few times. "Do you mind?" she asked as she pulled one out. "You want one?"

"No, but go right ahead. I'm good."

"Are you? Good?"

James gave her a hard stare for a moment before moving his attention back to the road, staying silent.

"Fair enough," she said, cracking her window and exhaling a cloud of smoke. "But I am quite good at reading people, and you, sir, have been way too tense. This is a road trip, and a road trip is freedom, man." Sofie paused a moment and looked at him. "Okay, okay, so maybe you think I'm crazy, but I can prove it. For instance, I just bet you I can guess a band that you like on the first try."

James glanced at Sofie, who was looking back expectantly. "Alright, I'll go along, if only to see that ego of yours deflate a little when you're wrong."

"Oh, I won't be wrong, just you wait and see."

"Okay, you're on. And the stakes... let's say, a soda or beverage of choice."

"Deal, you just have to be honest now. No lying, that's the only rule." Sofie adjusted in her seat, leaning with her back somewhat against the door, staring at James for a moment.

"Well, I'm waiting," James said as he glanced over at her.

"I'm getting there, don't worry. You are a tough one—but wait, I have it, I have it." She took a moment, searching through her phone. "Okay, here we go."

When the music started playing, James recognized it almost immediately, but he waited just a little while to keep her guessing, letting the guitar riff fully transition to a more comprehensive indie/alternative rock sound which spilled through the otherwise expectant silence within the car. "*The National*," James said the name slowly, pausing again for effect, as he looked over at Sofie, who was leaning toward him in expectation. "I'll admit it, you're pretty good."

"Yes!" Sofie slammed her palm on the dashboard. "Ha, I knew it. I told you, didn't I tell you?"

"Well, I mean it's not to say I *love* their music necessarily—"

"Oh no, you don't get to walk this back now. I can tell you like it."

"If you would let me finish, yes, it's good. I like it. Also, it has that feel which makes for good road music, doesn't it?"

"That it does, James, that it does." She noticed a slight smile come across his lips. "See, I had said you'd be happy I was here."

Over the next hour, neither of them said much, as they sat listening to the music and watching the scenery go by. The road cut across vast open wilderness vistas with mountain ranges rolling through, and very little civilization.

"Man, I think I could just drive through this forever. Just looking at the mountains and valleys pass by while listening to great music, couldn't you?" Sofie asked, while staring out her window.

"Yes, I think I could."

"Yukon is beautiful, different from Norway, but beautiful, you know. It has that unadulterated beauty that remains when humanity hasn't messed with it too much by replacing everything with steel towers and asphalt jungles. Ah, but then again, we wouldn't be out here in the middle of it without those things, would we? I think most of us have good intentions. It's just that we screw everything up in the end, regardless."

"Well, that is what we do best. Screw everything up."

Sofie lit another cigarette. "Are you sure?" she gestured with the box toward him. James shook his head. "Come on, live on the wild side a little."

"By smoking a cigarette?"

"Touché," Sofie laughed. "I see your point. Better not to ever start, anyway."

"Hey y'all, we're gonna be making a stop ahead," came Ray's voice over the radio.

A moment later James was following the Coupe and SUV into a parking area next to a lake. Ray, his fiancé Tehya, Marcos, Freddy, and Emily all got out of their vehicles and started walking down to the lake. Sofie hurried over to them and started talking to Tehya. Marcos hung back to talk to James, who was coming up behind them.

"How's the car ride so far?" Marcos elbowed James gently in the arm.

"It's fine," James said.

"I mean Sofie, she's something, isn't she?"

"I'm not sure what you mean."

"Uh-huh, sure you don't. It's gonna to be a long road trip is all, a lot of miles in the same car." Marcos gave him a sly smile and moved off towards the rest of the group.

The lake they were at was long and narrow, and the road followed along it for some ways. Along the shoreline, which comprised a gravelly dirt, the area was open and rocky. When looking away from the lake back across the road they were driving on, the ground rose and become cluttered with spruce and fir before rising still further up to the mountain's snow-topped peaks. The sky was partly cloudy, but the sun was shining now.

They stayed there for only about fifteen minutes, just long enough to stretch their legs, take a few pictures, and enjoy the beautiful view of the mountains which surrounded most of the lake. James stayed a little away from the rest of the group—partly out of habit, but mostly because he didn't trust them, especially after being lied to about having his car to himself, not believing for a moment that Ray merely *forgot* to mention Sofie. Watching them talk and laugh together, he felt very apprehensive about what the rest of this trip might entail. Soon, they all began walking toward their vehicles.

"So..." James said, once they had been on the road for a little while again, "why *are* you all going down to Vancouver?"

"Well, this has sort of become a thing over the past few years," Sofie said. "We do a road trip like this once or twice a year—plus or minus one or two of us, mind you—but the entire gang, more or less. It's not always the same spot, but Vancouver is probably our primary destination. We've all been there several times now. I don't know, there's just something about the road, don't you think? But this time *is* different... it will probably be our last road trip of this sort. That's because, well, let's see, Ray and Tehya are just headed down there as a vacation, but Marcs will catch a flight and be going all the way to Mexico, or was it just San Diego, I forget. But he is moving down there for good. I guess he finally got too sick of the cold. And then Freddy and Emily are moving to Vancouver permanently, as I may have mentioned before."

"And you," James prompted, when it sounded like Sofie might not continue.

"And me... I don't know. Ray, Tehya, Freddy, Emily, and Marcos are most of the friends I have in Whitehorse, so naturally I'm tagging along with them for as long as I'm able to. It'll be strange to lose so many of my friends all at the same time."

James stayed silent, keeping his gaze on the road.

"And how about you?" Sofie continued after a moment of silence. "Alaska not work out? How long were you up there for? And now you're headed back home, to... where did Ray say, Illinois?"

There was a space of silence again before James finally spoke. "Alaska. No, I wasn't there long. Not very long at all."

"Did she break your heart, or did you break hers?"

James glanced at her for a second, then said, "Why would you say... you know, I don't think I want to talk about this."

"But there was a woman, wasn't there?"

James stared out at the road in front of him.

"And she broke your heart, which is why your headed back to Illinois. I'm right, aren't I? I mean, if it was the other way around, you would still be up there, wouldn't you? And—"

"She died." James flung those two words out flatly but impatiently, as if simply in need of stopping Sofie's flurry of speech and using the only two words he had to make that happen.

Those two words seemed to still the very air within the car. There was a moment of silence. The music wasn't playing anymore, and although the constant hum of the engine remained steady as the car continued droning down the road, even that had seemed to disappear.

"Shit, I'm sorry. Sometimes I run my mouth too much, sorry. I guess that explains it, though."

"What does it explain?"

"Oh nothing, I shouldn't have said... just that, why you've seemed so melancholy. It makes sense now."

"Melancholy? Is that what you call it?"

"Well, you know what I mean. You've been reserved, quiet, sad or whatever, so yeah, melancholic. Now I know why."

James stayed silent as he motionlessly stared ahead at the road.

"I get that you probably just want me to shut up right now, but first I just need to say that if you ever want to talk about it, I'm here, even if it's just to have someone to sound off on."

James rigidly gripped the steering wheel. "I don't."

Sofie pulled another cigarette out and lit it as she cracked the window open, letting the roar of rushing air inside. Then she started looking through her phone for more music to listen to.

As they continued driving down Highway 1, the talk eventually returned to superfluous conversation. The terrain had flattened out now, and there weren't any more mountains in the visible distance, only the seemingly endless stretches of trees along either side of the road, still mostly conifer, but with some mixture of hardwoods as well.

After about ninety minutes, they all stopped at a gas station. It was small, like most of the others found scattered along the highway, nestled in the vast forests hundreds of miles away from any large city. The little wooden building sat in disrepair with its sagging roof and tattered shingles, as if it was trying to hide behind Its only gas pump which looked so old—in both style and accumulation of rust and peeling paint—that most who saw it would be surprised that it was still in working condition.

"What do you want me to get you?" James asked as they were both getting out of the car. "For your winning of our bet."

"Oh right. Umm, I'll have a beer," Sofie said.

"For in the car, really?"

"What, I'm not driving."

Everyone was out of the cars, some using the restrooms, and some were buying refreshments at a highly inflated price. After James finished pumping gas, he went inside to do the same.

When he came back outside, he stopped for a moment. In the parking lot, Ray and Sofie were talking a little way off from the gas pump.

"...You told me we weren't gonna be going back there. You gave me your word," Sofie was saying.

"Plans change, this was last minute," Ray said.

"Bullshit! You knew I wouldn't come along if we were going to make that stop again."

"Calm down, there's nothing to worry about. I've told you, it won't be like last—" Ray stopped abruptly, noticing James was staring at them.

Sofie looked back now as well, catching James's eye for a moment before turning back to him. "Fine.

Whatever Ray. It's not like I ever have a say in what happens, regardless, right?"

She started walking away from him, but Ray grabbed her arm, pulling her back toward him. He whispered something in her ear, and then let her go. She stared at Ray for a moment and then stalked off to the car, slamming the door shut as she got in.

James followed her and once again they were on the road behind the other two vehicles. James wanted to ask about the argument, but questioned whether this was the best time to ask. He had allowed himself to relax a little on the road, Sofie's exuberant personality disarming him a little, but now all of his paranoia and wariness were back in full force.

Sofie lit a cigarette in a stiff and abrupt manner, exhaling a puff of smoke out the open window. "Jævla fitte," Sofie spat out in her native Norwegian tongue. Sighing, she continued, "Ray's a great guy, but he can just be a genuine piece of work sometimes. This is supposed to be a vacation, and he has the gall to do something like this. Stykke dritt." She looked at James and then took another drag from her cigarette. "Ah, forget him. Fuck them all. We're still having a good time, right?"

"So what was that all about back there?"

Sofie gave him a hard stare with a clenched jaw, taut facial muscles, and narrowed brow. Then her face suddenly relaxed, the hard stern lines softening out, and she let out a sigh. "It's nothing. Really, just some personal baggage between the two of us, nothing you need to worry about. So, what did you get me?"

"Right." The abrupt change in Sofie's tone and manner startled James, and he couldn't shed this dark cloud which had invaded his thoughts. Just what was that argument really about? James reached back and brought up a bottle of Stella Artois, trying to sound unconcerned. "It's from Belgium... the closest thing to Norway I could find."

Sofie laughed, "It'll do, thank you." She popped the cap off with a lighter, then took a good tug from it. "Ahhh, now that's refreshing, you want any," she gestured with the bottle toward James.

"No, that's okay, I'm good."

"Ha, I wouldn't let you, anyway. After all, *you're driving*," she mocked. "There'll be plenty when we camp anyhow." A moment later she said, "We need some new music, and I think it's time that you guess."

"Guess what?"

"What kind of music I want to listen to? What *I* like."

"No, I don't want to guess. I'm not good at that kind of thing. Just play whatever you want."

"Oh, no-no, you don't get off that easy. That's not how the game works. I guessed first, so now it's your turn. Come on, just try it, it's fine if you're wrong. You'll just owe me another beer, is all. You even have a pretty good hint from what I've played earlier."

James sighed. "Well, there is that, I suppose." He begrudgingly played along and tried to put on a cheerful face, even if it was fake. "Well, if I go by *Team Me* and what else you've played... I don't know. I can't think of any Norwegian bands. Ummm, hmm... *Lana Del Rey*."

"Lana Del Rey," Sofie said the name real slow. "I don't think I know it."

"Well, I told you I wasn't any good at this, I didn't even want to—"

Sofie burst out laughing. "No, I'm sorry James. I know it, and I like her music. I even have it on my phone, so you win this round." A moment later, she found the music and started playing it.

Sofie sat staring out her window where snow-topped mountains once again appeared off in the distance "Oh yeah," she said, "I suppose I should mention we're going to be turning off on the Cassiar Highway instead of continuing down the Alcan. Not that it really matters to you, you'll just be following. But if you are interested... I don't have a map in front of me, but we'll be taking it all the way till it hits up with Highway 16 halfway down British Columbia, and then we'll continue making our way down to Vancouver."

"Thanks for the heads up. I appreciate it."

"No problem, anytime."

The Cassiar Highway. It hit James that so far, they'd been driving the same route he had driven on the way up less than a month ago. Once they turned off the Alaska Highway, everything would be new, as it would now be his first time traveling through this road. When he had first come up to Alaska, he had been driving north from the same city of Vancouver they were now headed to, but he had instead chosen to take the more eastern roadway up, which although might be slightly longer, went through Dawson Creek, where the Alaska Highway officially began, and then continued through Fort Nelson, Whitehorse, and into Alaska.

The whole route naturally seemed quite familiar so far, except for the fact, of course, that he was not driving alone anymore, and maybe the mountains had a little less snow on them. His entire state of mind was now different as well after everything that happened, and it almost seemed like he was a completely different person now.

He thought back to when he first met Elena, pulling her out of the water. How over the next few days he had tried to understand what she was going through, what she was keeping from him, and how to help her. Before he knew it, he had fallen for her, even when he finally found out about what Cole had done and the game he had drawn them both into. Despite all his efforts to save her, she still died. Even so, all of what happened during that fateful week with her still mattered, didn't it? And if it did, what was he supposed to do with it? What purpose did it serve—can it serve?

Images fluttered through James's head. A man moving toward him from the shadows. The same man calmly sitting on that rock, smoking a cigar. Pain, sorrow, anger, flowing through him in waves as he saw her lying there in the grass. *Her.* Elena. Falling into the water. Knife gripped in hand. That pleading expression on her face. Blood. *Don't forget about me—*

"*If you need to stop,*" came Ray's voice crackling through the radio, snapping James back into reality, "*this will be the last gas station for a while. Bathroom? Food? Otherwise, we'll push ahead.*"

Sofie grabbed the radio and looked at James for conformation. "Push ahead Ray, we don't need to stop any more than you."

They slowed down and turned south onto Highway 37—the Cassiar Highway—and past the gas station on the corner. "He seems to be almost in a hurry. Why is that?" James asked.

"Well, he's not really, but he has this idea in his head, 'When you're on the road, be on the road. Then when you get to your destination that much faster, you can put that extra time to better use,' is what he had told me once." Sofie had a slight smile when she glanced at James. "You get used to holding your bladder when traveling with Ray Neyati."

James smiled back. After a little while, he steered the conversation in another direction, asking, "You all seem to be a pretty tight group of friends, huh? I mean, with these frequent road trips, always as a group and everything, it's cool. How do you all know each other?"

"It all happened through Ray, I guess. We all knew him by one way or another, and then it was through him that we all met and got to be friends with each other as well."

"And the road trips? Do you all just sit around a table wondering what to do, before finally saying, 'well, where should we go this time? I don't know, maybe Vancouver for a third time,'" he said more derisively than intended.

"Look around you, James. Does anything you see show that just maybe taking a frequent road trip through this kind of country might be an appealing prospect?" Sofie's voice took on an increasingly bitter tone as she was talking, but now it had become distinctly sour as she said, "And so yeah! We go on a few road trips. Why the hell not? Perhaps we drive many of the same roads and stop at the same places. That means nothing. And yet you sit there with that accusatory tone, as if I'm conspiring against you with supposed lies and half-truths."

"I didn't mean anything..." He realized that his last comment may have been unnecessarily spiteful, and wasn't even sure why he had said it, but it surely didn't warrant the sudden flurry of sour hate flung at him in response.

"Yes, we take road trips. And it may be that Ray Neyati has a few diversified business opportunities that will occasionally take him quite some ways from Whitehorse." Sofie was staring out her side window, her words suddenly calm, yet still carrying a sour undercurrent. "So yeah, sometimes we'll combine a few business-related stops into these road trips. It only makes sense after all and doesn't really detract from the overall experience. We would almost be stupid not to, economically speaking, and we all try to help each other out when we can."

"Hey, I get it. I didn't mean to insinuate anything."

Sofie sighed, "Perhaps not."

CHAPTER 6

There was a definite difference between the Cassiar Highway they were now on and the Alaska Highway. This stretch of concrete was narrower and often made its path over hills and around tighter bends more than the previous road; a clear indication they were no longer on the primary artery of traffic any longer. A sign informed them they were now in British Columbia, and if James could tell if there was any difference at all from Yukon, it was that the forest seemed a little thicker and more prevalent here, although that might just be because of how the trees hugged closer into the shoulders of the road they were now on.

Darkness infringed upon his mind once more with the silence inside the car and the trees passing by. He felt almost tied down to these people now with Sofie riding with him, and he didn't know what was going to happen or what he should do. His original plan still seemed reasonable to him, though, of just making it down through Canada and then into Illinois. Once he was back home, or at least back in the United States, he would deal with detective Smith and what happened with Cole. Then, if they believed his story and didn't arrest him for Cole's death, he could try to get back to some form of normal life.

While these thoughts still preoccupied his mind, he heard Sofie say, "You know, you're kind of quiet, aren't you?"

His arms tensed, becoming rigid, and his jaw clenched up. *Of course she would be one to say something like that.* He had hoped that she was more intelligent than to ask whether he himself knew he had a quiet disposition, especially after he revealed that the woman he loved had died. Yet she had the gall to state that he was quiet. He said nothing, though, staring out ahead of him.

"Well, maybe we just need some different music. You choose."

"Whatever you want is fine with me."

"Okay, I get it; I'll have to read your mind once again. That's fine, just give me a moment."

The music was soft and more melancholic as the song *Thoughts,* by the band *Adna* played through the stereo.

Minutes passed by as he listened to the music, feeling himself relax a little and some of his tension start to ease. He glanced at her. "I guess you are good at this game."

She leaned back in her seat, closing her eyes. "See, I told you. I know you already, James."

They continued to drive, and now the silence that they drove on in was more comfortable than at any previous time of the trip, and James questioned whether he was wrong about Sofie after all.

"Hey-yo, Ray. I think we passed the spot." It was Freddy's voice coming through the radio.

"No, no, it's up ahead yet," Ray replied through the radio.

"Are you sure? I could've sworn it was back before that bend. I think we must've passed it."

"Come on now Freddy, I didn't pass it yet. I can recognize every tree here. I know exactly where we are, and I'm saying it's up ahead yet." And then, as if as an afterthought, Ray continued, *"You should really trust me more ol' boy. I've been through this road more than you have."*

Soon after this exchange, James saw brake lights in front of him as the two cars slowed down abruptly. They were turning off onto what in only the very loosest terms could be called a road. James noticed the absence of any signage as he turned into the very narrow grassy lane that cut through the forest. The vehicles crawled over several large humps, and a gap where the side mirrors just barely passed between two old towering pines on either side. Without warning, the dense woods gave way to a wide, gravelly shoreline of a lake. On the opposite side of this water, a mountain rose above the spruce covered shoreline, creating a view that belonged on a postcard. Next to a main highway, James expected to see such a lake surrounded by cottages, hotels, or at the very least a campground, but here there was only the natural landscape untrammeled by man. How much of British Columbia remained in such a state of untouched natural beauty?

"It's magnificent," James said as he gazed out across the lake.

"Ray knows what he's doing and where he's going on these trips. I'm not sure how he first discovered this spot, but it has become one of the usual stops along this route." Sofie saw the look of awe James had as he continued to stare out in front of him. "No doubt you can see why. This is just the beginning. When you're traveling with us, it will be a trip you'll never forget." She looked down for a moment before opening her door and exiting.

Ray and the other four were moving toward them. "Hey-hey-hey, I told you this would be great, didn't I Soph?" Ray said as he hugged Sofie. He looked at his watch, "Not even six o'clock and we've already arrived at our campsite, how do you like that James," he gave him a slap on the shoulder, "Just look at that view, man, it never gets old."

They were standing on a wide stony shoreline—which they parked their vehicles on—where the foot of the mountains came right up to the edge of the lake on three sides; the spruce covered slopes turning to bare rock with a few patches of remaining snow where the peaks reached into the sky. Behind them, the thick forest of spruce and pine stretched out like a green wall.

Over the next thirty or forty minutes, everyone was busy setting up their tents and establishing the campsite. James was just finishing up with his tent when he noticed Sofie was standing right behind him.

"What a beautiful tent you've got there," Sofie said, admiring how the gray-colored overhanging rain shield artfully covered the yellow body of the primary structure.

James looked over at the three tents that were set up a little way off from his own. "Which one is yours?"

Sofie followed James's gaze. "Umm..." she looked down at the ground now, "Well, that's the thing, see... you know how I was originally going to be driving along with Ray's brother, and well, one thing leads to another, and I'm a little embarrassed... The thing is, when I had to move my things over into Ray's SUV—of course I had a tent packed initially—but now I recall how it became a causality to having limited space in the transfer, and so my tent never followed with me."

"Oh. So, who's are you going to be sleeping in? Ray and Tehya's, theirs looks plenty big?"

Sofie let out a nervous laugh. "They do have enough room, true, and would, of course, let me if I asked. But well, they're gonna want to... well, you know. It might be a little awkward if I was there. Freddy and Emily would be the same issue, if there would even be room, which is doubtful. And then Marcs, well, you can see how small his tent is, along with other reasons."

James glanced over at his own spacious tent. "I see."

Sofie saw the frown on his face and how he was rubbing his brow. "Never mind, I never should've brought it up. I have a sleeping bag and Ray has a tarp I can use, so I'll sleep under the stars. It'll be better this way."

James looked at Sofie, running his fingers through his hair as he let out a sigh. Then he began rubbing the back of his neck in agitation.

"Well..." Sofie turned and began walking away.

"I'll take the tarp and sleep outside; you can have my tent," James suddenly said. "It looks to be a clear evening, anyway."

"That's not what I... shit, I never should've even brought it up."

"No, really, it's okay. I'll sleep outside and let's leave it at that." James started walking away.

"Fine then."

James was sitting on a rock close to the water's edge. He had a beer that he got from Ray, and the cigar he was smoking was half done. He was glad that Ray had dismissed any halfhearted offer he had made to help with preparing dinner, as he had only wanted to be by himself again, if only for a little while. Maybe he shouldn't have given up his tent. Was she just manipulating him, making him feel bad for her to get what she wanted? He wondered again what he was doing traveling with them and why they ever invited him along.

"Hey."

James flinched, looking back to see Sofie standing behind him. "Oh, hi. I didn't hear you."

"We got a fire going and we're cooking up some grub. You should come over and join us?"

"I will, in a little while."

"Well, okay then." Sofie stood there a moment with her hands folded in front of her, tapping a finger over her other hand, as if she wanted to say something more. Instead, she turned and walked away.

James took one last puff from his cigar before smearing the end against the rock to put it out. Taking one more look across the lake, he got up and walked back to where there was a good fire going with three-foot flames made from the nearby dead wood scattered over the forest floor. Above the fire hung a pot from a tripod of thick branches. Ray was taking the pot off the hanger and setting it on a rock nearby. Freddy, Emily, Sofie, and Ray were talking and laughing. Tehya and Marcos were also just now walking over from the lake where they had been working on something.

"Caribou stew, mmm, mmm, mmm," Ray said as he stirred the contents inside the pot. "It shouldn't be too much longer now." He carefully hung the pot back over the fire.

"Heads up, James," Marcos tossed him an ice-cold beer, grinning as James turned and barely caught it at the last second. "Well, what do you think?" Marcos swept his hand, gesturing toward the lake and mountains on the other side. "It's not so bad at all, is it, travelling with our little group of vagabonds?"

James took a moment to look around. Ray was standing by the fire, looking down at the pot of stew, Tehya behind with her arms wrapped around him, resting her head on his shoulder. Freddy telling a story that Emily and Sofie were laughing at. He looked at the mountains, the water, the spruce bordering the rocky shoreline. "No, it's not so bad."

They gathered around the fire now, sitting on sawed logs, Ray and Tehya sitting together, followed by Marcos, Freddy and Emily, Sofie, and then finally James. Ray was talking about what it must have been like here two hundred years ago. The hardship and beauty of a life lived solely off the land, the harsh long winters, and the joy that spring would bring with it. He continued to talk as he again took the pot of steaming stew off the fire.

"Think about the joy and the fulfillment that they would've felt when they would've been sitting around a fire—like we are now—but after a successful hunt, or a day harvesting crops, or building a house, or maybe on the trail travelling north to new territory." Ray was ladling stew into six large paper bowls, continuing to talk. "Sitting next to their brothers and sisters, those whom they knew intimately within their close-knit community of whom they depended on for their mutual survival. Living off what they made themselves through the sweat of their brows. And free... free to live how they wanted to live, free from any outside government, save their own, free from the system."

"Well sure, there's a certain romanticism to what you're describing," Emily interjected, "but it's also a living where one long drought, or a severely harsh winter, could dictate life from death. It's a hard life, and one where even the act of just surviving can be a fragile thing."

"Of course, and that's a valid point," Ray said, "but it only reinforces what I'm saying, that it's through this kind of harshness of life, where you can rise above it and truly appreciate the beauty of living without being bogged down by all the unnecessary complicated mess of our modern lives."

James took a spoonful of the stew, blowing on it before tasting it. "I don't mean to interrupt," James said, "but I just have to say that this stew is incredible."

"Oh, please do interrupt him," Marcos said as he crushed his beer can and got up to grab another one. "When Ray gets talking like this, he's liable to wax philosophically all night long."

"Oh, don't mind Marcs. He's just jealous because he has nothing intelligent to say," Ray said. They both started laughing.

As James filled his bowl a second time, he began listening to two different conversations simultaneously. Over to his left, Emily, Sofie, and Freddy were reminiscing about a previous time when they had been camping at this lake. All he caught from this conversation was something about a trout that Ray's brother Damian had caught, a turtle, a squirrel that had somehow become too curious, and how all three ended up as a meal that night. Tehya, off on his right, was talking with Ray and Marcs about some of the history that her people had in the area, and James could gather that she was primarily of Tlingit descent and belonged to the Kwanlin Dün First Nation.

"You're first nations as well, right Ray?" James said, cutting into their conversation.

"Ray is Métis," Tehya said, glancing at Ray.

Ray patted her hand, then looked at James. "Yes, and if I let her, Tehya will start going on and on about how the Métis are a distinct group of native people with a long and rich cultural history. But to put it simply, I'm just somebody of mixed European and Indigenous decent."

Tehya laughed. "Of course, it's a tad bit more complicated than that simple summation, though." There was a moment of silence before she again turned to Ray and said, "But hey, so we should probably do that thing before we lose any more light."

"Everything's ready, I assume." Ray replied.

"Naturally. I just need to grab my gun."

"Alright. Hey everyone, it's time to light the annual pyre."

James watched as most of the group dispersed toward the lake while Ray and Tehya went to their vehicle. Sofie, who had initially begun walking toward the lake, came back to where James remained standing.

"Come on, you're gonna want to see this." Sofie touched his arm, motioning him forward with her.

They were standing in front of what appeared to be some sort of makeshift raft constructed of large sticks tied together to form a rectangular, flat base. Above the base, sticks and brush formed a triangular tepee like structure. The whole thing measured about three feet wide at the base and was five feet high. Nestled between the branches near the top, James noticed an orange-colored cylindrical container, which also had orange flagging tied onto branches directly around it, making the container stand out even more. Ray came up with a gas can and poured gasoline over the entire structure. Tehya was behind him carrying a scoped bolt-action rifle.

It was dusk, and the sun, which had long since dipped behind the mountains to the west, was now setting behind the hidden horizon. Daylight was fading fast, and already it was fairly dark.

"Every year we do this," Ray said, mainly speaking toward James but also to the entire group. "Anything we have going on in our lives that we want to rid ourselves of, we ceremonially put to fire in this way. It can be a physical object of some sort, a letter, or even just a silent prayer mentally laid upon this pyre soon to be consumed in fire."

James watched as every person walked up and laid some memento upon the raft, most of which were just folded up sheets of paper, presumably describing some vice or issue which its author sought to purge. Freddy laid a pair of old leather boots down on the edge of the raft. Then Sofie stepped forward, hanging a necklace over one of the sticks. He noticed that Ray seemed to give her a strange look as she did this. She caught his look for a moment and then quickly stepped back.

"James, is there anything you would like to set upon our pyre?" asked Ray.

James glanced at Ray, then looked over to Sofie, who was again standing at his side. There was an odd look in her eyes that he couldn't decipher. After a moment, he stepped forward. Hesitantly, he reached out his hand, placing it upon the branches wet with gasoline. He closed his eyes, and then after a moment stepped back again to where he previously stood. He felt Sofie's hand rest on the back of his shoulder.

Ray and Marcs pushed the raft out into the water. They all stood and watched as it slowly drifted farther from shore. Tehya stepped forward in front of everyone, shouldering the rifle and looking down the scope. She stood there like this, poised for the shot.

"Can you still see your mark, babe? I know it's pretty dark now?" Ray asked.

"I can see it—I can see it. Just be quiet."

In another moment, there was a ringing bang from the gun, immediately followed by a louder boom as the top of the pyramid-like structure floating on the water exploded, igniting the rest of the raft in flames.

There was some cheering on the shoreline, and then they all became silent, watching as the pyre burned away in the growing darkness before breaking apart and falling into the water.

The campfire was freshly stocked up again and everyone was once more seated around, watching the flames.

"Freddy, go pull the car up here and turn on some music, will ya?" Ray said as he tossed Freddy the keys. "Play something jazzy, and with a good beat."

Freddy put a on a mix mostly comprising 1950s rockabilly music.

Ray started grooving to the music. "Now that's the stuff, Freddy boy!"

"Yeah, yeah, I know what you like. I've been traveling with you long enough now," Freddy said in a subdued tone.

"Oh, come on, you sourpuss," Emily said as she got up, letting the music move her. "I know it's been growing on you and that you secretly dig it. Come on hon, dance with me a little."

"Em, you know I'll always dance with you, no matter what the music is."

The fire continued to burn as they fed more wood to it, and the night deepened as the stars illuminated the sky. James sat where he was, continuing to drink more beers, watching some of the dancing that went on between Freddy and Emily, and Ray and Tehya. He enjoyed listening to the conversations that rarely pulled him into the dialogue, and he felt that perhaps this was better than remaining alone, and there wasn't really anything so strange to worry about with these people. Cradling his half empty Kokanee beer between his hands, he sat staring into the flickering flames of the fire, watching it change and seem to morph in shape and character. He saw the house atop the bluff; the flames licking up its side, consuming the darkness it held inside. Or was it releasing it out into the world? He could see *her* in the flames, the knife, the blood. The debt he still owed her to make her sacrifice matter.

"James, tell us, what do you think?"

"I just don't think that Niccolò Machiavelli is the person to look to for moral advice," interjected Emily.

"I'm not saying that we should look to his book *The Prince* in that manner, or that I even agree with much of what he says," Ray replied. "But in this at least he is right, that choosing a side is always better than neutrality. Wouldn't you agree, James?"

"Choosing a side?"

"You will always be respected as a genuine friend or as a genuine enemy. Machiavelli points out that if, say, you have two neighbors that go to war with each other, if you stay neutral, in the end both sides will feel betrayed, the winner will not want halfhearted friends that don't fight with him, and the loser won't respect you anymore either. Now if you were to pick a side and fight earnestly, even if that side lost, you would still have a genuine friend, and in this way, it would go better for you than if you had stayed neutral."

"There's some sense in that," James said. "I don't know if I ever thought of it that way before."

"Always choose a side. That's what I'm saying. Loyalty, stick by your friends, and fight for what you believe in when the time comes. Nobody likes a Switzerland, James, remember that."

"Alright honey, I'm sure he gets the idea." Tehya said as she patted Ray on the leg and got up to get two more beers from the cooler. "Let's not get too serious on a night like this," she sat back down, giving a beer to Ray.

Several conversations seemed to go on again, and James must have zoned out once more, when he again heard his name called out.

"—James, what do you think? Do you get it? Can you figure it out?"

"What?"

"The joke," Sofie said, "or I guess it's more like a riddle, maybe. I don't know, a joke—riddle?"

James stared at her. "Umm, could you repeat it once more?"

"Two penguins are canoeing in the desert. One penguin asks the other, 'where's the paddle?' the other penguin answers, 'Sure does.'"

"I don't get it," James replied after some pause.

"I didn't get it either when I first heard it," Tehya said. "Don't worry, even when you do, it's still kinda stupid."

"I don't know, I think it's kind of cute," Emily retorted. "It's clever, you know."

"You're just saying that because you got the answer right away when you heard it," replied Ray.

"Well, maybe in part, but can't I gloat a little? I never get those kinds of jokes right away?"

"Of course you can, and you would be right to do it," Freddy said as he kissed Emily on the cheek. "They're just salty because they didn't get it."

"Come on, two penguins canoeing in the desert, one says, 'where's the paddle?', the other answers, 'sure does.'"

James took another swig of his beer. "I give up."

"Ok, so here's a hint. Just put the word *it* before the sentence."

"Tehya!" Sofie exclaimed. "That basically just gives it away. I was going to give him more time to figure it out."

"It where's the paddle? I still don't get—oh okay, yeah, I get it now. It wears the paddle. That is stupid," James said.

"You're just saying that because you didn't get it," Sofie stated. "It's a good joke... riddle... whatever. At least Emily agrees with me."

James huddled closer to the fire as the wind seemed to pick up. He looked up at the sky and saw that most of the stars were now concealed by clouds.

"Well, me and Emily are gonna hit the sack," Freddy said, "Night all."

"I think we're going to call it a night as well," Ray said as he and Tehya got up.

Marcs soon followed suit and made his way to his tent as well.

When they were the last ones left at the fire, Sofie asked James, "You still planning on sleeping outside? It's going to rain tonight, probably will start any minute by the feel of this wind."

"It's fine. I'll cover myself with the tarp. It's not a big deal."

"Really? Because that tent is plenty big for two and—"
"I'm fine, Sofie."

"Okay, Okay." She threw her hands up in the air, "Just don't say I never offered, or that I took your tent from you."

James got into his sleeping bag, pulling the tarp over him just as a few raindrops started to fall. When he closed his eyes, he tried to keep the dreams from the previous night out of his head. Images of skin peeling off Elena's rotting face. He hoped those dreams wouldn't come back as he tried to focus on other images. Of mountains, and rolling green forests, of winding blue rivers and lakes such as the one he was at now.

CHAPTER 7

James was sitting along the edge of the lake in the dawn's early light, relishing this moment of solitude. His thoughts drifted as he looked out across the water. He remembered how Elena and he had run toward Cole's house that night expecting to catch him unawares, but he had caught them instead. Of how he stood in the chilly night air, Elena remaining quiet by his side as they listened to Cole as he said, "One of you can walk away from here, one of you can't. Now is the time, choose." He was about to run for the knife himself when Elena pulled him back. Now she was gone, and he remained, faced with the weight of figuring out how to move on after such an event. He could still hear her voice pleading out to him in the dark, "This can still mean something. It's up to you to do the right thing."

The sound of raised voices broke James away from his thoughts, and he looked over at the campsite, where he saw Sofie and Ray arguing again. Sofie was moving her arms about as if to emphasize what she was saying. As James got nearer to the campfire, he could start to hear what she was saying.

"But if the situation has only worsened, why would we be going back there?"

"I've told you, it has no bearing on our visit," Ray said, his arms crossed as he faced her.

"*Bullshit* it has no bearing. I know you Ray, and I know how close the two of you are. And why did you ever invite *him* along with us if we were going to be doing this? Oh, never mind, why waste my breath. You lied to me before, you'll just lie to me again." She turned, rushing away, her eyes flashing at James as she quickly continued toward the tent with exaggerated movement.

"Better pack up, we're going to be hitting the road again in about half an hour," Ray said as James approached the campfire. "If you want anything to eat, make it quick." Ray gave James a peculiar look, as if he was wondering how much of their conversation he had overheard.

Not feeling hungry, he went and packed up his sleeping bag.

When everyone else seemed to be about ready, he got into the car, turning on the two-way radio and sat back in his seat to wait. When he heard the door open, it quite surprised him to see Marcos, and not Sofie, getting into his passenger's seat. Of course, why should he expect Sofie to be riding along with him the whole way? It was rational that other people would ride along with him, wasn't it? Yet he *had* expected to spend the entire drive down with Sofie in the passenger's seat, and now he found himself resenting Marcos for being there instead.

"Hey buddy," Marcos said. "I guess I'm going to be riding along with you for a little while. Sofie seems rather pissed right now. What did you say to her?"

"Me?"

The SUV in front of James started moving. "*Alright—alright—alright, back on the road again, and the freedom of tires rolling across the vast stretches of pavement,*" came Ray's voice through the radio.

It was only a moment before Marcos continued to say, "I wouldn't worry about it, though. You know women, they're always pissed about something or another, right? Hell, man, it's probably even a good sign. She's just playing hard to get."

"Okay, why are you so interested in my personal life, and especially this supposed interest I have in Sofie, who I didn't even know before yesterday?"

"Hey man, she's hot, so yeah, naturally you're interested, and I saw her getting out of your tent this morning, so don't put up any false modesty with me. I didn't think you'd move this fast, but I'm impressed. So, tell me, did you seal the deal?"

"What? First of all, I slept outside under a tarp and let her have the tent, and no, it's not like that. She—"

"Ah, playing the gallant angle huh, that might work too. Don't sweat it bro, like I said, this whole acting mad thing is a good sign, and can all work to your advantage. You just have to play it right, and tonight could be the night." Marcos was searching through the radio for stations. "Man, nothing good's coming in." Then he landed on a station playing a variety of rock. "This will do, I guess."

It was quiet for some time, and then James brought up the subject of Sofie again. "Why is it you seem to think that everyone's always sleeping with each other?"

"Well, because in my experience, they usually are," Marcos said as he laughed.

"In that case, why don't you go after her? I mean, you seem to be so interested in who she may be seeing."

"Hey, don't think I haven't tried, but she was more interested in a certain Neyati at the time."

"Wait, Sofie and Ray?"

"She isn't really my type anyway," Marcos continued, as if not noticing James's comment. "And Norway? I'm heading back to Mexico, so I don't need to hook up with some ice queen. Nothing personal or anything, she's a cool chick and all, I just prefer a Hispanic you know, with—"

"Sofie and Ray were a thing?"

"Well, that was before him and Tehya were official, and I'm not sure what all went on between them, but as you can see, everything seems copasetic now, and Sofie is free to mingle and... well, you know."

For the next hour, Marcos talked on and off about his plans once he got into Mexico. How he found this incredible little place to rent, and how he and his brother who he hasn't seen for three years were going to run this food truck together, and that he would be perfectly happy if he never saw snow again for the rest of his life. He also pressed James for information on his time in Alaska.

"I just don't want to talk about it, that's all," James said, determined not to discuss why he was leaving Alaska.

"Fair enough. We all have a right to our own secrets."

"It's not secrets, I just don't want—"

"*Listen up now. I just want to let you know that we'll be stopping at the Bell 2 for some grub, which is about five kilometers ahead.*"

The Bell 2 was a full-service lodge and restaurant with heli-skiing in the winter. The interplay of white stucco and log walls of this green roofed building gave it an aesthetic both modern and rustic. On arrival, they filled up the vehicles with gas and then parked.

"Hey, and don't worry about Sofie. I've got your back, bro. She'll be back in your car for the rest of the day. I'll work things out for ya," Marcos gave James a friendly shove with his fist against his shoulder.

The seven of them sat at a table in the restaurant where they had a beautiful view of the mountains and enjoyed good food. Sofie was quiet throughout the meal, but otherwise, the chatter was lively, and things seemed normal.

As James entered his own car, he saw Sofie talking to Ray and Marcos. A minute later, Sofie parted from them and was heading toward James's car. Sure enough, Marcos was right, and Sofie was going to be riding along with him again. He found himself unable to suppress a small amount of happiness toward this new arrangement, although he quickly attributed this to his mild dislike of Marcos, and not perhaps a growing fondness toward Sofie.

As Sofie entered his car once again, he noticed her angry disposition as she glanced at him, saying nothing. She crossed her arms, and every movement she made seemed jerky and forced. How she would constantly adjust her position in the seat, or how she would keep bringing her hand up to her face to bite her nails before catching herself and abruptly placing them back in her lap again. It created an uneasy tension between them, and James couldn't help himself from taking brief glances at her.

"What?" she finally said. "Stop looking at me. You're supposed to be driving."

"What, no... it's just that I meant to ask. Marcos, I thought he would be riding with me for the entire day?"

"Oh, that. Yeah, he said you couldn't shut up about some emu farm you were working at in Alaska."

"Emu's?" James couldn't help suppressing a laugh.

"Yeah, I don't know what the real reason was, but I wouldn't take it personally."

James thought that would've been enough to ease the tension, but Sofie became quiet again and seemed deep in thought. "Is there something going on?"

Sofie looked at him and then let out a sigh, running her hands through her hair. "First, I just want to say that I had no part in bringing you into all of this. I had no idea Ray had even brought you along until the morning we left. Of course, I had no problem with it—why would I—even if this was the first time we brought an outsider with us, and on the spur of the moment, no less. What I still can't understand, though, is why Ray would invite you if he was planning to go back there all along?"

"What are you talking about?"

"It's just... I had asked him weeks ago whether we would make that usual stop along the way, and he assured me—promised me even—that we wouldn't. We had all decided that we would stay away from them after what had happened last time, that we wouldn't get involved with their disputes. I wouldn't have even come along this time if I knew."

"Sofie! What in the world are you talking about? We are going to Vancouver, aren't we?"

"Yes, we are going to Vancouver. However, Ray wanted me to let you know we are going to be making a brief stop first. Just a short business stop, or would it be a social visit? I'm not too sure exactly, but I guess it's a bit of both." Sofie was tapping her fist on the handle of her door. "Do you ever get that feeling deep down within your core that says something just isn't right? Look, I don't know what's going to go down, probably nothing, but he still never should've involved you in it." She paused for a moment and looked at James. "Gunnar's not such a bad dude, though. And I'm actually looking forward to seeing Chloe again. We've been down to his place many times now and do some business with him. We're going to be spending the night there, and that should be alright, I mean, there's no real reason to think that anything will go..." Sofie kicked the floor in front of her. "But why? Why are we going back now, with everything that's going on with them?" Letting out a sigh, she now looked over at James, giving him a kind of apologetic smile. "Never mind my paranoid ramblings, don't listen to me. I don't know what I'm talking about. Everything will be fine, I'm sure."

James didn't respond. He began to fit a few pieces together in his head, the fragmented bits from the arguments he had overheard making more sense. What he still needed to figure out was what his part was in all of this, and why he was invited. He sat back, pondering what she had said in his head, and listened to the music.

After a while, James picked up the radio. "Hey Ray, pull over."

"*What was that? Say again,*" Ray said.

"Pull over!"

"*Right now, on the side of the road. Why?*"

"Just pull over—we just need to switch drivers real quick."

A moment later, both vehicles in front of them pulled to the side of the road and stopped.

"I can't drive anymore right now. Take over Sofie," James said after they stopped. Without waiting for a response, he got out of the car and made his way over to the passenger side.

Sofie got out after a moment, looking James in the eye as she passed him, making her way around the car, not about to question why.

When James settled into the passenger's seat, he took the radio again and said, "Alright, good to go."

"Right on, right on."

Sofie, now driving, followed behind Ray and Freddy's vehicles, and a random mix of music continued to play through the stereo speakers. James leaned back in his seat and closed his eyes. For a long time, no one spoke.

Then, after a while, James ventured to ask, "What is it you were talking about before? Why w*as* I invited to travel along with you?"

"I don't know, James, I just really don't know. There's probably no reason at all."

"That's not how you made it sound before. What's really going on here?"

There was a pause before Sofie answered. "This man we're going to visit, Gunnar; he and Ray go way back. Ray's been friends with this guy for a long time, and doing business with him for almost as long, I think. He does seem like a stand-up guy, eccentricities aside, it's just... whenever we were there, it seemed almost like we were in another world altogether. It's as if they live their lives completely insulated from the rest of the world, and nothing from the outside has any effect on what they do. It's odd, because in some ways I'm almost glad to be going back once more."

"Sofie... you're not making any sense. One minute you're all distressed and talking like there's some ominous reason for returning there, and the next it's all soft reminiscence and kind words about this guy. I just don't get it. I mean, what kind of business dealings does Ray have with this guy?"

"It'll be fine." Sofie seemed to say it to herself as much as to James. "Everything'll be fine. It will all work out. It has to."

Sofie didn't seem to want to talk about it anymore, and after a while, James closed his eyes again, this time falling asleep.

CHAPTER 8

"James. James wake up. We're here."

Here. James opened his eyes and looked around out of his window. It was dark, but the last hint of twilight still hung in the sky. He could hear the gravel crunch under the tires and saw the vehicles ahead of them illuminated in their headlights as they slowly drove up the narrow drive where the trees encroached heavily on either side. Soon the driveway opened into a clearing, and they were pulling off into a grassy area next to several other parked vehicles.

This was it, the place Sofie had been talking about, their stop along the way that Sofie at least didn't think they should be making. It made him think of Cole and his house with his twisted game, and everything that happened with Elena. No, this wasn't like that. Nothing like that was going to happen here. Surely, this was a completely different situation. When he got out of his car, he could faintly hear music coming from the direction of the house, at least the reverberating beat of the bass. All he could see of the building from the parking area was the garage, the rest being obscured by trees. He walked up next to Sofie and grabbed his car keys. Ray and the others came over from their vehicles.

"Well, James, I'm not sure what Sofie told you..." Ray shot a hard glance at Sofie, then continued, "but we're going to be staying here for a night, maybe two. Gunnar is an old friend of mine, and I just couldn't allow myself to make this trip down here without making a little social call." Ray put his arm around James's shoulder. Walking across the drive, Ray continued in a lower voice, "Now I know you didn't expect this minor detour in our trip, but just give it a chance, and I'm sure you'll enjoy your time here. Sofie, whatever she told you... well, she sometimes exaggerates things, so don't take it too seriously. I told you before we left you wouldn't regret traveling with us, and I tell you again now, you won't. Besides, it appears there's a party going on tonight, so have a few drinks and socialize a bit. This'll be fun, just you wait."

Despite what Ray was saying, James got a sense from the tone in how he said it, that he also viewed this entire visit to an old friend as something more serious than what he was letting on.

They walked along a path that led behind the garage and was bordered by a wall of tall and narrow juniper trees. Many small lights emanating from the ground illuminated the ornate brick path they were walking on.

James paused briefly where the trees ended, as he caught his first view of the house in the darkening light. It was a single-story structure of a modern architectural design, with a flat slanting roof broken up into different sections, the siding a combination of brick and wood.

Sofie moved next to James. He could see a look of apprehension on her face. "What kind of a situation have you gotten me involved in?" James asked her.

"What? No, it should be fine. I'm sure everything has settled down since our last visit."

"Last visit?"

"Shhh, it's nothing. Hurry." They were trailing behind the rest of the group, and Sofie tugged his arm as she hurried to catch back up with the others.

The brick path led to a covered stone entryway, where two men were standing arrayed in trench coats and fedoras. Right behind them were two AR-15 assault rifles set against the wall.

"Well, well... Ray *'Frankie Sixes'* Neyati, and company," the man to the left of the door said. He then started scraping the heel of his boot on the stone floor for what seemed like at least twenty seconds as he eyed the group with an askance stare before he finally continued. "Gee, it's good to see you again. The boss is inside, but he might be busy."

"Thanks Cory," Ray said. Eyeing the weapon against the wall, he added, "Over cautious as always, are we?"

"Shit, you know how Gunnar gets," Cory said. Then, as Ray went inside, he focused his attention on the rest of the group as they walked past him. "Emily, Freddy, hey I haven't seen you in a while, Marcos. Sofie..." he eyed her from head to toe as she went past, "always a pleasure."

"Only in your dreams, Cory," Sofie replied with a smile.

"And what pleasant dreams they are, Miss. Ah, but who's this now, not someone else who has claimed that pleasure, I hope?"

Sofie glanced back. "This is James," she paused, before adding in a more playful tone, "and he doesn't have to dream." She grabbed his hand, pulling him with her before he could say anything, rushing through the door.

James saw that Sofie was laughing slightly as she let go of his hand once they were inside. The deafening volume of the music washed over him like the crash of a wave, which mainly comprised of a heavy bass beat, backed up with a slow guitar rhythm beneath it, and every so often there was this deep ominous singing which James couldn't understand. He was standing in a wide, spacious room with vaulted ceilings. The wood flooring stained almost black was matched by the wooden supports stretching across above. The off-white of the plastered walls offset the dark coloring of the wood. In the center of this room was a large circular stone fireplace, its base raised about two feet from the ground, with a metal chimney suspended directly above. Immense glass windows lined the opposite wall from him along the front of the house, reflecting the fire and silhouettes of the people inside. The room seemed to be filled with smoke, not from the fireplace by the smell—a mix of cigarettes and marijuana—which hung about in a haze and seemed somehow to shroud everything about him.

"It might be a while before we can talk to him, I don't know," Ray yelled over the music to James and Sofie. "Sofie, look after James."

"I can handle myself," James said with a hard look and narrowed brow, first at Ray, and then Sofie.

"Alright, I meant no offense. We'll be around, and enjoy yourselves while we're here, okay?" Ray gave Sofie a look, and then drifted toward a group sitting around a table, yelling out greetings and shaking hands. The others soon dispersed into other parts of the room, leaving James and Sofie to themselves.

James saw that Sofie was still looking at him. "I meant what I said. I don't need a babysitter."

"Are you sure about that? I get a sense that you might be a little out of your element here."

James brushed past her, moving to a bar that was situated near the end of the expansive glass wall and adjacent to a kitchen area. He went behind the counter and grabbed a bottle, pouring himself a glass of Bourbon. "All this is free? People just help themselves?"

"Yup, that is—kind of, yes." Sofie leaned against the bar, running her hand over the glossy walnut surface. "It's an open bar, self-service." She raised a hand to stop him from pouring her a glass. "I'm not a real big fan of bourbon. Here, I have a better idea. Just give me a second."

James took a sip from his glass, looking over the place again as Sofie started mixing a drink. There seemed to be about twenty people in the room, not including Ray's crew. Gathered around the nearby kitchen counter there was a small group passing around a joint. They all appeared to be in their thirties and a little rough around the edges, the men with scruffy beards, the women casually dressed and not done up in makeup. Several brown leather sofas were staggered around the fireplace, and on one of these there was a young couple who were making out. A few others were talking—or more like yelling, their Canadian accents rising over the music.

The one thing that stood out most in the entire room was a high-backed, deep brown leather armchair, framed in wood with intricately carved designs. It sat isolated at the other end of the room, facing two vast panes of glass that stood for the corner walls of the house. James could only see the back of the chair from where he stood, but just then an arm appeared off the side from some figure seated, unseen. It was a strong, masculine arm, which, after making a slight gesture, had receded out of view again. A tall, thin man with a receding hairline and narrow mustache, who had been leaning against the wall, now walked up to the chair. The tall figure leaned down, listened, nodded, and then made his way across the room toward the kitchen.

"Here you are, mister." Sofie handed him a glass full of some dark drink with ice. "It's something that Tehya introduced me to that she calls a black Yukon sucker punch." She took a long drink from her own glass of which looked to be the same as what she gave James.

James took a swig from his glass. "Hot damn," he said, coughing. "What's in this?"

"Something to knock your socks off, and then some." She gave James a mischievous smile.

"I don't understand you, Sofie. It seemed like only a minute ago you were all worried and speaking ominously about coming here. Did you have some sudden change of heart about this visit or something?"

"No, it's just... why worry about things you have no control over," Sofie said, sipping from her glass. She noticed that James's gaze was soon drifting back to the solitary armchair across the room and had to touch his arm to get his attention again. "You know, James, whatever the reason you're here, I'm—"

"What? The music, I can't hear," James yelled.

"I'm saying that I've enjoyed your company on the road, whatever the reason for your—" She cut herself short as the music abruptly stopped, and different music started playing. A song by Johnny Cash, *Ain't No Grave*.

They both looked over and watched as the dark armchair slowly swung around and James finally saw him. His head was shaved bald except for a dark beard that hung down a foot below his face. He had broad shoulders, big arms, and even sitting down, he was tall. He wore jeans and a brown and grey-black flannel shirt with his sleeves partially rolled up and heavy brown boots.

James and Sofie walked over to where Ray and the rest of their group were now standing between the fireplace and the imposing figure sitting in his chair.

James could see the beginnings of a tattoo going up his left arm. He sat there with a still and unmoving face, but his dark brown eyes shone forth with a wild fire as he watched them. Everything was absolutely quiet except Johnny Cash singing, "*There ain't no grave, can hold my body down.*"

James stirred uneasily on his feet, glancing about at the others next to him, suddenly unsure of what to do with his hands before stuffing them awkwardly in his pockets.

The man slowly snapped his fingers, as if to the music. He closed his eyes and then moved his head slowly up and down whilst continuing to snap his fingers. As the song came near its end, he stopped snapping his fingers and opened his eyes, gazing out with a dark intensity. He shot his right arm out to the side and gave one last snap. The music stopped; silence filled the space.

The man suddenly burst into a deep, guttural and robust laugh. He slapped both hands against the armrests of the chair and sprung to his feet, standing even taller than James had first guessed. "I'm sorry, I just love that song. Ray Neyati, ha, I'm so glad you could make it. How are you, old friend?" He walked up with a broad smile across his face as he embraced Ray, patting him on the back like a friend, long missed.

"It's great to be back, Gunnar," Ray said, as he stepped back from the embrace.

"Come, come, let's get a drink," Gunnar's voice was deep and commanding. Walking over to the bar, he yelled over his shoulder, "Larry! Music!" He gave a twirling motion with his hand. Momentarily, music went back on—a mix of classic country similar to Johnny Cash—and now at a quieter, more reasonable volume.

James couldn't help thinking that Gunnar resembled a stereotypical lumberjack as he watched him, or perhaps more like a leader of some cult group. Either appeared just as likely.

They followed Gunnar to the bar, where he lined up eight shot glasses in a row and quickly filled them with an amber colored liquor. "Here's to old friends, not seen nearly often enough." He downed the shot with the rest of them, the sound of the small glasses slamming against the bar top as they all finished. Gunnar filled the shot glasses just as quickly a second time, waiting for everyone to pick theirs up again. "And once again, because why the hell not." He let out a guttural laugh, followed by the sound of glass against bar-top once again. "Man, and all of you are here, I'm so glad." He looked at each of them, his gaze settling on James with a curious look in his eyes. "Except for your brother, of course. His absence is missed."

"Alas, yes, his demons have finally caught up with him, it seems," Ray said. Then, noticing Gunnar's lingering gaze, "And this is our newcomer, James, who I had mentioned over the phone."

"Of course. It's so good to meet you, James," Gunnar extended his hand out. "I'm glad you can join us tonight. You're traveling in good company with Neyati here." He then shifted his attention to the entire group, saying, "Now you'll have to excuse me briefly, as I have a few things to discuss with Neyati privately. Afterwards, we can all sit down and catch up properly. So please, enjoy yourselves."

Once the two of them were gone, Marcos said that he was going to mingle and went over by another group of people. Freddy and Emily soon also drifted off somewhere together, leaving only Sofie, James, and Tehya still near the bar.

"So, James, what'd you think?" Tehya asked. "He's quite the guy, huh?"

"Gunnar, yeah, sure." James took a sip from the drink he still had. "There's definitely a presence about him."

"Hmm, that's one way to put it."

"Tehya, if you weren't engaged to Ray, I might think you have a thing for him," Sofie said.

"What, I can find the man attractive and still not intend to sleep with him, Soph. I mean, I bet every woman here would jump at the chance to be with him, as no doubt many have tried. Are you saying that you're really not at all interested? I hear he's still single, so you might still have a shot."

"No, I'm not. At least not after the last time we were here."

"Ha, fair enough."

James saw them share a knowing look between each other, and then sip at their drinks in the ensuing silence. "So hey," James said, "why did those guys outside the door have assault rifles? I mean, that is a little weird, right?"

Sofie looked at Tehya, giving her another strange look.

Tehya sighed, "Well, there's this group of people that live in the woods with whom Gunnar has had a long running dispute with. It's this new community that people around here have named, *the village*."

"Although *village* might not be the most accurate term," Sofie said, cutting in. "More like a bunch of people that decided to dress up and play ancient Indians—no offense Tehya—living primitively in the woods and cutting themselves off from the rest of civilization."

Tehya smiled. "Yes, thank you Sofie. She means in how it's all aboriginal people, first nations like myself. Only these people have decided to go and try to live in the way their ancestors had lived for hundreds of years. The idea being that they live off only what they gather and make use of in the surrounding area, no modern tools, electricity, or anything not fashioned themselves. I can understand the appeal to some extent, but it does seem a little extreme, perhaps."

"This would all be fine and well, of course," added Sofie, "live and let live and all that, except now some of their activities have been having a direct effect on Gunnar personally. Last year they were doing some prescribed burning, and it got away from them, turning into an all-out crown fire that consumed half of Gunnar's own timber and destroyed several houses belonging to some of his employees. Suffice to say, tensions have been rising."

"Yes, and of course his wife leaving him for none other than the chief of this same village hasn't exactly helped to ease matters any either."

"What?" James exclaimed, "Wait, so you're saying that Gunnar's wife left him for the leader of a group of people that he's having a major dispute with? Or is that what started this whole dispute in the first place?"

"It's hard to say what may have been going on before that, but his wife leaving does seem like the point when things really started to sour between them."

"Yeah, well it doesn't really matter though, does it?" Sofie said as she looked at her empty glass. "I need another drink. James, finish yours up, and Tehya can mix us up another one of those Yukon sucker punch drinks. Do you mind?"

"No, that's fine. But you mix them just as well as me, you know, nor am I the inventor of the drink as you appear to suppose."

"But you are the one who introduced it to me, so that's all that matters. And it always tastes better when you mix it so... James, give me your—"

"I'm good actually, I don't think I want anymore."

"You sure? One never knows what tomorrow brings after all," Sofie said, holding out her hand to take his glass.

"I said I'm good." He slammed his glass on the bar top.

Sofie raised her hands up momentarily and took a step back. Turning, she leaned against the bar and watched the other people about the room.

After a moment, James moved a little closer to Sofie and asked in a quiet voice, "So what exactly is it you're worried about, with being here?"

"It's nothing. It's probably nothing."

"It really is nothing, Sofie." Tehya. finished mixing the drinks, pushing one forward. "You can trust Ray. Whatever Gunnar's intentions may be, Ray's not going to let us get involved with some war that isn't ours."

"War?" James's voice let out quietly.

"Oh, don't mind me," Tehya said. "I can be rather dramatic at times, just like Sofie here. It's really not as bad as all that, so don't let our loose talk bother you. We'll stay here briefly and enjoy Gunnar's unbeatable hospitality and be on our way again."

"So, is it always like this here? I mean with these... parties or whatever this is, or is this just—"

"What you have to understand is that this is a small close-knit community," Sofie cut in, "and at the heart of it there's Gunnar who holds it all together."

"Or in other words, yes and no," Tehya said. "Gatherings like this are fairly common from my understanding, but they don't happen every week."

"Well, well, come on then ladies, gentlemen," Gunnar's voice boomed out, as he entered the room again with Ray behind him, "Let's get outside then, as we have some merchandise to unload."

"Really, we're going to do this tonight... in the dark? I thought we were going to wait till tomorrow," Tehya said to Sofie.

"I assumed so as well, but I guess the boss doesn't want to wait."

James, along with the rest of Ray's group except for Freddy and Emily, who didn't appear to be around, followed Gunnar outside, along with four other individuals from inside the house. They all gathered around Ray's SUV, where Ray, Tehya, Marcos, and Sofie proceeded to unload items from the back. Somebody started a car up and moved it, so that its headlights illuminated the area they were working in. After they almost entirely unpacked the car, Ray lifted a portion of the floor up. From this compartment, they removed numerous cases and stacked them in front of where Gunnar was standing. Four dark-colored cases of a heavy-duty plastic material stacked five feet high now stood ominously in the glow of the headlights.

James glanced at Sofie, who was standing near him again and staring ahead, expressionless. Things were piecing together in his head, Sofie's vague hints about why they were coming here, Ray's diversified business dealings, the conflict Gunnar was having with another community. He was getting a more complete picture now, but his own role in any of it still escaped him.

"Boys!" Gunnar snapped his fingers. "Bring these cases into the basement."

Four men came over and grabbed the cases, heading back to the house. Sofie went over now to help repack the car. James continued to stand where he was, alone, trying to figure out what he was going to do.

After the car was repacked, Gunnar walked back to the house. James regrouped with the others as they followed him. Sofie seemed to dislike the situation almost as much as James did himself, but he knew he still couldn't trust her. He grabbed Sofie's arm, turning her toward him as they walked. "Sofie..."

Sofie sighed, shrugging her arm away. "Not now."

Just before heading through the door, Gunnar stopped. Turning toward them, he said, "Please follow me to the basement if you would, where we can talk over a few things and then you can all get back to the party."

Once descending the stairs, they found themselves in a big open room that no doubt took up the major portion of the basement. Next to the landing was a large rectangular wooden table with eight chairs surrounding it. Off toward the other end of the room were a few couches, a tv, pool table, and a ping-pong table.

"Sofie!" a girl was running toward them, almost knocking Sofie over as she embraced her. "I'm so glad to—I didn't know you were coming."

"Oh, Chloe! I was wondering where you were hiding."

"I have something you just have to see—once you have time, of course. I'm sorry if I disturbed you, Daddy," the girl said, now turning to Gunnar.

"Not at all, dear. We'll just be a moment here." Gunnar walked up to Chloe. "I'm sorry that more of your friends weren't able to make it. You're not too terribly bored, I hope."

"It's fine, me and Cassie have found enough to keep ourselves busy."

"Of course you have."

"I'll come and find you as soon as we're done here," Sofie said as she rubbed the top of Chloe's head playfully. "I can't wait."

"You better." Chloe was then running off as quickly as she had arrived.

James watched all this with great interest. The girl appeared to be somewhere around twelve to fourteen years old, had auburn hair which was tied back into a ponytail. Her obvious affection toward Sofie was intriguing. He saw now that Gunnar was greeting everyone personally before they sat down.

"Now, where did Fred and Emily run off to?" Gunnar said after he had greeted Sofie.

"Who knows? I'm sorry, you know how... unsociable they can be sometimes," Ray said.

"Yes, well... Mike!" Gunnar yelled to the thin man nearby who James had previously seen being beckoned to that dark armchair before. "Mike, go find those two and get them down here. This involves everyone. And where are those sandwiches? There's supposed to be sandwiches down here. Our guests are hungry no doubt, go and find them some food. Get some beer down here as well, will you?"

"Yes, of course, sir, it'll be done." The man was then gone in a hurry up the stairs.

"My apologies, everything is in rather a disorder at the moment, but it will be remedied." Gunnar's eyes met James, and he gave him a long hard stare for a moment, before addressing the entire group, "Well, sit down, sit down, and we will come to order."

After everyone took a seat, Freddy and Emily came hurriedly down the stairs, apologizing for being late and finding seats. Right behind them was Mike, carrying a platter of finger sandwiches, and another man was behind him with a case of beer.

Marcos grabbed both a sandwich and a beer, and then Freddy hesitantly did the same.

"I want to thank all of you once more for being here," Gunnar said, as he sat at the head of the table, "I

131

know that many of you may have been a little apprehensive about coming back here after your last visit, so first let me just apologize for any... inhospitality I may have shown, and I will try to allay any concerns that you may have. That was a difficult time for me, and I didn't deal with the news I had just received very well. It happened to be a very ill-timed visit for you, but that doesn't excuse my behavior. Unfortunately, tensions have only increased since you were last here, but as I have told Neyati, I have no desire to get any of you wrapped up in our ongoing personal affairs. Our problems are our own. You are welcome to stay here for the night, or as long as you want, and I will enjoy your company and treat you like the honored guests you are. All of us here are grateful for the supplies that you have brought, and it may be that you have brought them at a very opportune time. There is a rumor circulating that within *the village* there is a sickness of some sort that has broken out. Now, if this is true, which I cannot be certain of, these supplies may be invaluable to them and be the bargaining chip we need in our ongoing negotiations."

Gunnar paused, taking a drink from his glass of scotch, then continued, "If this sickness is real, this could give us the upper hand we need. We have a problem however, all face-to-face talks between our two groups of people have completely ceased, as we have both unleashed rash words against each other, and now we are unable to even speak with them. We seem to be entrenched in a kind of stalemate, and they seem completely unwilling to budge in their demands. Now it may be that some of you might be able to help with this if you so choose ... being the closest thing I have to a neutral party, you may be able to mediate between both parties and get a discussion going again at the very least. Ray and Tehya especially, being of their race.

"We can talk it over tomorrow, and in the meantime, you can think on it. I've taken up enough of your time for tonight though, so go, enjoy the night, drink, have fun. We'll talk more tomorrow." He slammed his fist on the table. "Let's rock!"

Sofie walked off in the direction the girl had run off in, presumably her room. Ray and the rest were walking back up the stairs, and James decided to follow behind.

"One moment, James," Gunnar said, placing a hand on his shoulder.

James saw Sofie look back at him, wrinkling her brow, before continuing across the room. "Yes?"

"We haven't had a chance to talk yet, just you and me."

"No, we haven't."

"Here, let's go outside for a minute." They walked across the room to where there was a glass patio door leading outside.

The house was built into a hill where half of the basement was underground, but along the front it led out to the ground level. Outside, there was a stone patio with a fire ring where there was currently a blazing fire burning. Two people were sitting around it, but when they saw Gunnar approaching, they got up and went inside.

"Here, take a seat," Gunnar motioned to one of the chairs around the fire as he sat down himself. "You're from Alaska, is that right?"

"No, not exactly."

"As you may or may not have gathered, I run a logging business, among other endeavors," Gunnar said, seeming to disregard James's comment. "One that I have inherited from my father, and from his father before him. Logging runs through my veins; it runs through this entire community. All these people here at my house right now, they are almost all of them my employees. But more than that, they are my friends, and they have put just as much blood, sweat, and tears into this organization as I have. The logging industry may not be what it was a hundred years ago, and there are always new challenges to contend with, but I would never give it up. Sure, I've also diversified into other areas of business as well, but logging has always been the heart which sustains this entire region."

"You seem like a real pillar of this community, and I'm sure these people are very grateful for what you've done for them," James replied, not sure where this conversation was going.

"Be that as it may, now there's this other group of people, this gathering of various first nations people that have built their little town bordering near my own land. I gave no thought to this initially. If they don't bother me, I have no problem with them. But they come here, and now, after only a few years, they are trying to force me out. *Me* out!" Gunnar yelled, slamming his fist on his leg. "It's not enough that they burned down half the timber on my own property. Now they're taking away my forest tenure that allows me to log much of the surrounding public forest land."

Gunnar paused, took another drink of his scotch, and noticed that James looked a little confused. "No doubt you as an American don't understand how logging here in Canada works, as things are done different here than in the United States. The vast majority of forested land here in British Columbia is public land owned and governed by this province. This provincial government then offers forest tenures for the logging rights of much of this land. I have had the forest tenure for most of the surrounding area for many years now, always working with and abiding by their rules and regulations. My forest tenure had recently come up for renewal, and now I hear that without reason they are not renewing it and instead giving it over to a logging company affiliated with the Kitsumkalum First Nation of the Tsimshian people. This had happened a few months ago, just before Ray and them were here last time. When I asked the chief of *the village*, Kallik, about this, he didn't even deny his own involvement. He straight out told me that this was Tsimshian land, and it was about time that their people had a chance to profit off their own timber if they wished to."

James looked at him but remained silent.

"My family has been here for generations, much longer than many of the people that now reside in that village. What of my rights? I will not stand and let them take everything away from me."

"This is all very interesting, but... what does any of it have to do with me?"

Gunnar took a moment before asking, "Why do you think Neyati brought you along with him?"

James stared back at him. "Perhaps we had become good friends."

Gunnar laughed at this, and then in a moment his face became stern and serious again. "Ah yes, and what are friends for, in the end?"

James gave him a crooked smile. "Well, perhaps we just cut to the part where you ask what it is that you want from me."

"Being such good friends with Ray as you say, undoubtedly you would do what you could to help him out then."

"In what way?"

"But a genuine friend would not ask. He would act without question."

"It would seem that I'm not that kind of friend."

"It would seem that you're not a friend at all." Gunnar's voice now took a deep unnerving tone. "Let's drop this pretense then and be honest with each other. I'll repeat, why do you think Neyati brought you along with him?"

James started to wipe his sweating palms on the legs of his jeans, but paused abruptly when he saw that Gunnar was watching his actions. He quickly folded his hands together in his lap and said, "Why don't you tell me?"

"That's not an answer—"

"I don't know."

Gunnar let a smile spread across the corners of his mouth, the light of the flickering fire dancing in his eyes. He grabbed a stick and stirred the wood in the fire pit. "What I had said earlier wasn't quite true, about Ray or Tehya being able to broker negotiations with the people of the village. Kallik and his people know they are my friends, that they are loyal to me. That they are, in many ways, my people. But *you*, you are different. You're a true outsider. I think they would talk to you—no, in fact, I know they would. You could pretend to be on their side in this whole dispute. You could convince them to accept a new agreement where no one else could."

"Let's just say for a moment that I could do what you're asking. What isn't explained is why I would do it? I have nothing to do with what's going on here."

"But that's where you're wrong, James. The moment you decided to join with Ray's group as they traveled down here, you implicated yourself in their affairs. Take this merchandise that they delivered here today. You're just as much an accomplice as any of them in their actions now."

James thought about the cases that were unloaded from Ray's car, and what he might now be involved in. "What exactly is that *merchandise,* then?"

"Don't tell me you don't know. Care to give a guess?" When it seemed clear James wasn't going to say anything, he said, "Drugs." A hint of a smile came across his face as if he could read what James was thinking. "Pharmaceuticals, antibiotics, and medicine of the like." He paused, but James remained silent and so he continued, "The market for various medications and medical supplies outside of the restrictions and control of the government and the pharmaceutical industrial complex is larger than most realize. You get out to places like this, and many people don't want to be a part of the system, or just not have to sit and wait for treatment until it might be too late for them. Ray is someone who has connections with people who can get these products for actual cost and not the insane markup they would charge at hospitals."

"So, you don't supply recreational drugs, then?" James ventured hesitantly.

Gunnar let out a long laugh. "Like cocaine or heroin, oh I supply some of that as well. If there's a need, I'll supply it. I'm a man of the community, after all. What I'm most concerned with though is providing people with certain medical treatments without having to go through hospitals and big pharma. This is also something I hope to be invaluable when it comes to our negotiations with the village as well." After another pause, he said, "We've talked enough for now. We'll speak again tomorrow. Now go up and enjoy the rest of the night."

As James came back up into the main room, he walked straight to the bar, pouring himself a glass of bourbon, downing a big gulp. The music was back to being as loud as when they had first arrived.

"I see you changed your mind about that drink," Sofie said as she came up to him.

James shot her a hard glare, narrowing his brow.

"Was it that bad? What did he say—does he want you to do something?"

"It doesn't matter," he said, taking another drink.

The guests had begun to dance. Everyone was drunk, high, or both, and seemed to be enjoying themselves.

"Do ya want'a dance?" Sofie asked James, slurring her words.

She was leaning toward him; her face was flush as if from excitement. He got the sense that she just wanted to have a little fun and lose herself in the music and alcohol. She didn't need his sour mood standing in the way of her enjoyment. "Sorry, not tonight."

"Tehya, how 'bout you? Your man seems to have disappeared again."

"Umm, sure, I can't leave my girl hanging after all, now can I?"

James stood against the wall, watching all the people dancing, touching, drinking, and... his head was throbbing. The music was too loud; he had drank too much, and there was the question of why was he there. After Elena, Cole, and everything that happened back in Alaska, he was now here with Gunnar asking for his help, casting vague threats about what may happen if he refused. He closed his eyes for a moment, feeling the alcoholic buzz hum in his mind, then watched as Sofie danced opposite of Tehya. His mind flashed back to that night when he and Elena had danced in front of the fireplace, how the flickering light and shadow had danced across the swaying form of her body. Tomorrow, it would be over. As soon as he got up, he would leave. He would leave this house, leave Ray, Sofie and everyone else and be on the road again, by himself.

"Hey bro, there you are. How's it going, man?"

James looked up, startled, and saw Marcos in front of him, as if he appeared from nowhere. "It's fine," he answered after a moment, trying to come back to reality.

"It's fine?" Marcos motioned him over to a more secluded area of the room. "Bro, it should be great, not fine. So, what's up?" He followed James's gaze to where Sofie was dancing with Tehya. "You're killing me, man. Why the hell aren't you out there dancing with her? Why is she dancing with *Tehya*, of all people?"

James didn't answer, but he could feel his anger rising.

"The time is ripe; this is when you make your move. She's right in front of you James, go and dance with her. What are you waiting for?"

"Enough Marcos! Why do you even care? Just leave me alone already, okay!"

Marcos stared at him for some time, appearing somewhat startled. "I'm sorry. I just thought that you liked her and I was trying to help. I guess I was wrong," he said, turning to walk away.

James looked about the room for Ray or Gunnar to figure out what his sleeping arrangements would be, more than ready to have this night over with and be back on the road again.

CHAPTER 9

"Get up. James, wake up."

James opened his eyes as someone was shaking his shoulders.

"James, I think I could use your help."

Fighting the sleep out of his eyes, James tried to focus his vision on the figure in front of him, but it was dark and hard to see. His head ached, and he felt like he might puke, being somewhere in the transitional period between drunkenness and hung over. "What?"

"Meet me outside, I need to talk to you. And be quiet, don't wake anyone," the voice whispered.

"Sofie?" James said as recognition of the voice came to him, but she seemed to be gone already. *What could it be now?* As sleep continued to leave him, he recollected where he was, and how Gunnar had apologized for not having any rooms available to use when he was shown one of the couches in the basement where he could sleep. James searched his hazy memories of the prior night but couldn't remember much after his conversation with Gunnar. He fumbled his hands along the ground until he found his shoes, then, putting on his jacket, he carefully made his way through the dark shadows about the room in the direction where he faintly remembered the stairs being in. There were several other people strewn across the room, sleeping on a cot or a couch, as he made his way to the stairs and then out of the house. He followed the illuminated path of solar lights along the ground, looking around for Sofie.

"James, over here."

James looked over to where the voice came from, seeing the dark silhouette of a person standing at the end of the driveway near the vehicles. He made his way over. "Sofie? What is this? Why are you dragging me out here in the middle of the night? What time is it even?"

"I'm sorry, it's just... something has happened. Everything is moving so fast I hardly know what's going on myself, but... well, a little while ago I heard a knock on my door—I was sleeping in one of the guest rooms—and someone slid this letter into my room. Here, it's probably easiest if you just read it." Sofie handed him a folded sheet of paper.

"I can't see—"

"Here," Sofie handed him a flashlight.

With the beam of the flashlight, James read the letter.

Sofie,

I'm sorry I can't talk to you in person. I fear you would only try to prevent my going. But I know I can trust you not to tell Father of what I now here write. After last winter, I count you as a dear friend, and am confident you feel the same. I know what Father is liable to do if this situation doesn't get settled soon. There may be something that I can do about this, though. I am going to see Mother, but I think I could really use your help. I'm already on my way, but if you're willing, meet me at that spot we know. You know, under the borealis.

Your friend, Chloe

James handed the letter back to her. "Okay, so what does this have to do with me?"

"I don't know what she plans on doing, but I think she's out of her depth here. I'm going to help her, and I'm wondering if you would come with me."

James was quiet for a long moment. The moon shone out through a gap in the clouds, and he could see the apprehension evident on Sofie's face. "Come with you? To find the girl, and then what?"

"We help Chloe do whatever it is she's trying to do."

"But... why come to me for help with this? Why not Ray, or Tehya, or any of the others?"

"Because Tehya, Marcos, Freddy, and Emily, they're all loyal to Ray, and Ray is loyal to Gunnar." Sofie's voice was rising. "Normally I adore such loyalty, but in this case, it means I cannot turn to any of them, because I can only be beholden to Chloe in this, and not Gunnar or anyone else. They might see this as a betrayal of sorts, and I don't want to put them in that position. You're the only one I can trust to not get anyone else involved. You're the one I trust to help me here."

James was silent, contemplating the situation in his head.

"There is a war that could start here at any moment between these two groups. Chloe is asking me to help her try to stop it. I'm asking for you to help as well."

"And you think that you can stop a war?"

"To try, yes. But more so, to at least help a girl who finds herself in a situation so much larger than herself."

"Why do you even care? Who is this girl to you?"

"You're right, I wanted nothing to do with this conflict involving Gunnar's people. That's why I didn't want to come back here again, because I knew that something like this was going to happen. That he would somehow rope Ray into his problems. But now I'm involved." Sofie waved the letter in front of her. "I care because Chloe chose me as the one person in this entire world that she trusts to help her above anybody else in this situation. I clearly formed a bond with this girl during my last visit, which is stronger than I even realized, and because she asked this of me, yeah, I'll do whatever humanly possible to help her. And also, because I wouldn't be able to live with myself if I let her down now." Sofie took a step closer to James. "So, come with me, James, and let's do something that really matters."

"This isn't my fight, though. I only have a few pieces of information to go off of in understanding this conflict, and now I'm just supposed to trust that you and this Chloe are the ones who are doing the right thing, the ones I'm supposed to side with. What could I even do if I did go with you?"

"I'm not asking you to take a side. I'm asking for your help. I'm asking because... well, because I'm scared. I have no idea what I'm getting into or how far this will go. I realize that we both don't know each other very well, but after spending two full days in a car together, I think you can see enough of someone's quality to get a sense of what he's made of. I know you are looking for something, some meaning, purpose. So, what do you say?"

James stared at her, a shadowy figure four feet away. Darkness now concealed her face, but he heard everything he needed to in her voice and knew what she expected him to say. After a period of silence, he finally said, "I'm sorry. Whatever it is that's going on here, I don't want any part of it. If you have the hubris of thinking that you can stop a war, then fine, that's your business. I'm leaving. In fact, I think I'm going to leave right now, because I've had enough. I have no part in any of this. You said before that you could fit all your stuff in Ray's car if you had to, so do that. I'm getting out of here."

"Really?" Sofie asked, taking a step back from him. "Well, if that's the way you feel, then you really should leave. I just need to get my bag out of your car, and then you can be on your way."

They both walked over to James's car without saying another word. Once James unlocked the doors, Sofie opened the passenger side and, after briefly rummaging through the mess inside, she came out with a few bags, which she then put into Ray's vehicle. Sofie walked back over to where she previously was standing and grabbed a large backpack from off the ground that James hadn't seen before, slinging it over her shoulders. It was a fully decked out backpacking pack.

"Well, I guess this is it then," James said, and then walked over to the driver's side of his car.

"Yup. Guess so." Then, right as he was going to open his door, she called out, "James... I hope you find what you're looking for."

James stood for a moment, looking down. He opened his door with a motion of getting in, when he again paused, "Sofie... I just want to say that... it wasn't bad, having you as a passenger while on the road."

Sofie remained silent this time.

"Okay," James hopped into the driver's seat and closed the door. He turned the key, buckled his seat belt, put the car in reverse, backed out of the parking space, and pulled forward down the driveway. Looking in his rearview mirror, he saw the dark shape of Sofie still standing there like she had been, staring at the car as he drove away. He continued to watch her until she disappeared into the night.

He made his way slowly down the long narrow driveway that he had come up less than twelve hours earlier. It struck him then that he didn't even know where exactly he was. He had been asleep when they arrived here.

He stopped the car where the driveway met the road. Looking down at his phone, he saw he didn't have any service. He went to his paper maps, only to remember he didn't have any specific to British Columbia, only Canada as a whole. After unfolding enough of the map to see the whole of British Columbia only to find that everything was too small to be of any help, and not knowing enough about where he was, he crumpled the paper into a ball and threw it to the side. Focusing on a recent recollection, he seemed to remember Sofie saying that this detour was off to the West. Or was that all in his head? He couldn't remember. He looked at the compass in his car, which read south-east. If he turned left, it should take him east and hopefully back to the Cassier Highway. That is, if they hadn't turned off onto several other roads along the way, and who knew which direction the road may ultimately lead. His head would spin with variables and indecision if he let it, and in the end, all that mattered was that he drove and put as many miles between this house and himself as he could. North-east was a better start than south-west, so he turned left.

James rubbed the back of his neck, his gaze darting about the trees at either side of the road. His head hurt, and he felt nauseous from the beginnings of a hangover, and there was an ache deep within his gut, a gnawing feeling of guilt. He played out the convenient excuses for why he was leaving through his head. *It's not my problem. I don't know what's even going on there. How can she expect me to help? I can't be roped into a situation like this that I don't even understand. I won't be, not again.* In trying to quiet these thoughts, he played some music, the song *Shallows,* by *Daughter,* which had a kind of sad and dark indie folk sound to it. He watched the lines of the road in his headlights race by as he listened.

Images visualized in his mind erratically—waves crashing upon rocks—the sun setting over the mountains across the bay—walking through an old growth pine forest. He could see that house, as when he had first arrived there, sitting isolated along that Alaskan coastline, warm and inviting, seemingly perfect. This image dissolved into one of water—a scream—a splash—falling. A woman running in the darkness of night. She was there in front of him now, smiling in the sunlight, brushing her blonde hair out of her face as the wind blew through it. A moment later, a man sitting in the dark, his face in shadow. Then, the other house, situated upon the bluff, ominous in the moonlight. Elena again, her face sad and almost pleading as she looked at him in the dark woods, "If this is the end, I don't want it to end like this," she was saying. "Why do we never do the things that we really want to do? Why do we always wait too long, until there isn't any time left?"

James gripped the steering wheel tighter as he continued to drive along the curves of the road whilst these images and memories were continuing to play through his head. "Shut up. Get out of my head!" James shouted.

The fragile, ethereal female voice continued through the speakers, *If you leave, when I go. Find me, in the shallows.* The images cycled by, faster now, Elena slowly dancing in front of the fireplace—Walking along the shoreline—the feeling of her hand in his—a wall of fire—peering down over a cliff into the darkness of water—running—a knife— "Don't forget about me James"—falling—blood—darkness—yellow lines running across blacktop—deer—

A deer—standing in the road motionless—staring right at his oncoming car. James reacted—too late— slamming on the brakes and swerving to his right. Wheels squealed on pavement as the car slammed into the hind legs of the deer, sending it tumbling over the left side of the hood and back onto the road. The car went skidding off the gravel shoulder, sliding down into the ditch before crashing head on into a tree.

James looked at the now deflated airbag from the steering wheel, breathing in the dust hanging about the cabin of the car, which gave off a strange mildew and smokey scent. His adrenaline was pumping and he felt a bit dazed, but otherwise, he seemed to be uninjured. He opened the door and got out, noticing the bent-up hood and indentation of the tree around the front bumper. He stumbled up through the long wet grass from the ditch onto the road, still a little bewildered by the impact. The moon was shining between sparse clouds, casting the road in soft illumination. Fifteen yards away, James saw the deer lying on the road.

He could see the deer trying to get up with its front legs, as the hind legs remained limp. It struggled on the pavement, even managing to drag itself forward a little before collapsing back down in exhaustion. James walked up to it, seeing that its hindquarters were all bloody where the car had hit it. The deer lifted its head up, looking at him, then struggled again to move. "I'm sorry. I'm so sorry, big guy," James said under his breath.

James turned, walking back to the car. *I'll have to shoot it, I guess, poor thing. Shit, that's right, I don't have my gun anymore. So now what?* James stopped next to his car, noticing for the first time that there was some blood streaked across the hood and driver's side door. *Just leave it. What else am I supposed to do if I can't shoot it?* James tried to turn his mind to other thoughts, figuring he would just sleep in his car until morning when he could hitch a ride to somewhere with cell service and call for a tow. Or he could head back to...

James looked back up the road, thinking about the deer again. He pounded his fist against the car once. "Fine. I'll do it," he said, opening the door.

A minute later, James was walking back up to the road gripping a large Bowie style knife in his right hand and a flashlight in the other. The deer had made its way a few feet from where James had last left it, as it lay to the side of the road now. James knelt at the deer's side, gently petting its fur. The deer was shaking. James noticed he was also shaking a little. O*kay, this is way more personal than a gun. I wish I never threw it away.* James took a long deep breath and then brought the knife up, resting the tip of the blade where the heart and other vital organs were located. "Don't worry big guy, everything'll be alright. Just one more quick moment of suffering before the end."

The deer twisted its head back to look at him before letting it rest on the ground again. James stared out ahead of him, to where the road blended with darkness. Then, with all of his weight, he plunged the knife down. He felt the blade slide in up to the hilt of the knife, and immediately the deer bucked up against him. With its last reserve of energy, the deer struggled wildly to get away. It was all James could do to lay on top of the deer, trying to keep it down, and the knife staying pressed tightly into it. Even so, the deer still managed to move a foot or two with James on top of it. Wheezing and breathing hard, the deer's struggling started to subside, and soon stopped moving all together. Throughout this struggle, James had kept his gaze out toward the road. He remained motionless on top of the deer for a little while after it had stopped its movement. James couldn't hear any breathing coming from the deer, and everything was still and silent. "There. There now."

James slowly lifted himself off the dead deer, pulling the knife out as he did. His eyes were moist as he looked back down the road toward his car.

What the hell? James froze.

Not more than fifteen yards away from him, in the middle of the road, stood a person. In the dark, he couldn't make out any more than that. Remembering that he was carrying a flashlight, he shined the beam of light at the figure.

She brought a hand up to her face, blocking the light. Then a beam of light shone into James's eyes, making him look away for a moment. When he looked back, he saw the girl running across the road and into the edge of where the trees began. "Wait, don't run! I'm a friend of Sofie's," James yelled, not sure of what to say or do. He saw her beam of light pause, dart around sporadically a few times, and then move deeper into the forest.

James stood there a moment longer, trying to comprehend what had just happened and what it could mean. Words Sofie said to him flashed in his mind, "I think she's out of her depth here. I'm going to help her." He ran to his car, opening the door and digging through his cluttered belongings. He was barely even aware of what he was doing, only that he had to act. He had to hurry, while there was still time, before she got too far. James slung a backpack over his shoulders, slamming the door closed behind him and ran across the road into the woods where he had seen Chloe disappear into.

CHAPTER 10

Sofie stood, looking out at the car until it disappeared down the driveway. She was wearing a gray-colored jacket that she had just grabbed from James's car, as well as jeans and a pair of sturdy black boots that came halfway up to her knees. She pulled on a grey knit beanie snugly over her head, feeling the chill of the night breeze. Then she adjusted the straps of the large hiking backpack, which was fully equipped to sustain her for several days out in the wilderness. Turning around, she walked across the open clearing and toward the edge of the woods. Sofie walked along the tree line, darting her flashlight back and forth across the trees, and soon was turning again to walk back to where she had come from. "Come on, come on, it has to be here somewhere. Why does all this look so different than before?" *Well, last time it wasn't dark outside for starters, and then there was snow on the ground,* her mind answered. "It doesn't matter. The trail has to be here somewhere."

She was walking past the same patch of woods for the third time when her light finally flitted across a definite gap in the trees. It was a clear trail, and although nothing looked distinctly familiar, her sheer force of will, if nothing else, convinced her that she was now on the right path.

Following a defined path, her mind was now free to roam. *Stupid. How could you be so foolish, Soph? I can't believe you stooped so low as to practically beg for that fool's help. Maybe if he better understood my need to help Chloe, his answer would've been different... but it doesn't matter.* "Fuck him. Fuck everyone. I don't need his help. I don't need anyone's help." Her mind drifted back to the winter, when they had last visited Gunnar's place and she had been able to connect with Chloe.

They were all huddled next to the blazing central fireplace in Gunnar's house, as the wind outside beat against the walls of the house and blew the falling snow horizontally against the windows. Ray, Tehya, Marcos, Freddy, Emily, Sofie, and Ray's brother Damian were talking together amongst themselves.

"I don't like this situation any more than the rest of you," Ray was saying. "And I have no desire to get wrapped up in this dispute, but with this snowstorm, we should wait till tomorrow at least to leave. Even if the roads were clear, it's already midafternoon, so let's make the most of it and settle in for another night. Just try to keep your distance from Gunnar if you can."

Sofie ventured off on her own and soon found her way into the basement. Toward the far end of the main room, she saw Chloe playing a game of pool by herself. Sofie walked up and watched her play for a minute before asking, "Care to play against an opponent?"

"Sure," Chloe responded, barely glancing at Sofie.

"I rarely ever get the chance to play, so I probably won't be much of a challenge."

"No matter," Chloe said as she racked up the billiard balls for a new game.

Sofie glanced toward the ceiling, hearing the voices above them. "So, do you play often?" she asked as she took the break shot.

"I guess."

They took a few turns back and forth as Chloe quickly took a commanding lead.

The voices above them were getting louder, and they could hear Gunnar shouting. "I don't care what the prudent course of action is! Who does that whore think she is? It's not enough for her to burn my forest down, she has to take *my* logging contracts away as well. The bitch won't stop until I'm utterly ruined! I tell you I'll be dead before I let her get away with it!" Glass shattered on the floor above their heads.

Sofie felt sympathetic as she looked at the girl who was concentrating on her next shot, pretending not to hear what was going on above them. "Does he get like this very often?"

Chloe paused mid-shot, giving Sofie a hard stare. "Like what?" she asked, then made her shot.

"Never mind." She shifted uneasily on her feet, glancing about the room, hating how they had to pretend that nothing was happening, and not knowing what to say. She just wanted to get away from all of it, wishing they could be back on the road. As she looked at the girl across from her, she couldn't help wanting to get her away from it as well.

The game ended with Chloe decisively sinking the eight ball into the corner pocket. Sofie saw Gunnar's brother cross the far side of the room, entering a small secondary kitchen.

She went over to talk to him. "Caleb, I don't think Chloe should see her father like this. I mean, it's still the early afternoon, and he's already this bad?"

Caleb frowned. "Yeah, I know, I agree. I would take her to my place, but I should really stay here and look after my brother."

"Does he get like this very often?"

"No. Never before his wife left him, and then, while he has found his way to the bottle with increasing frequency after that, it has rarely ever been bad like this as far as I'm aware."

"Isn't there somewhere she could go? I can see how much she hates this."

Caleb was deep in thought for a moment. "Well, there is one thing you could maybe do. You two seem to get along pretty good, and well, it may seem a bit odd, but if I know my niece, it may be just what she needs. What would you say to taking Chloe out camping for the night?"

"Camping, like in a tent? That seems a little extreme, and with the snow..."

"The snow should subside soon, and we have all the equipment, even a small heater. What, you've never been winter camping before?"

"I have, and well... why not, I guess. It's better than staying here."

"Great, I can get you two fully loaded out."

"Alright, I'll go and ask Chloe if this is something she would want to do." Sofie went to look for the girl.

She found her in her bedroom, sitting on her bed with her back to the wall and headphones on, listening to music. Sofie sat next to her, and after a moment asked, "What are you listening to?"

A shrug of the shoulders was the only response Chloe gave.

Sofie reached over and removed the headphones from her head. "What do you say we get out of here for a little while?"

"What do mean?"

"Well, I happened to hear that there's a certain lake nearby which you may be partial to, and right now your uncle Caleb is loading up two sleds so that you and I can go on a little overnight camping trip."

Chloe's face lit up. "Wait... so we're going camping, like right now? Just the two of us?"

"Yup. So, what do you say, want to spend the night in the bitter cold open sky with little old Sofie?"

"Umm... yes!" Chloe exclaimed, before flinging herself toward Sofie and giving her a quick embrace. Then she darted to the door, pausing only to say, "I better get out there and make sure uncle Caleb doesn't forget anything."

They were blazing along a small river in their two snowmobiles, Chloe out in front leading the way. The river opened into a wide, snow-covered lake, where not a single other person was present. Sofie rode up alongside of Chloe and stopped.

"It's beautiful, isn't it?" Chloe asked, as the snow was now dwindling to only a few flurries.

"Sure is. So, where do you want to set up camp?"

"Follow me." Chloe closed her visor, throttled down on the gas, and flew across the lake.

They stopped on the lake a little out from a rock cliff which rose some fifteen feet above that portion of the shoreline and provided some protection from the west breeze that was even now beginning to subside. The tent was up in little time and after a brief foray into the woods to collect firewood; they were back at their campsite building the fire. The sun had set, and the first few stars began appearing in the darkening sky as the clouds above were scattering.

Sofie huddled close to the fire once they had a good blaze going, feeling the temperature drop and thinking that she should've put on yet another layer of clothing and being grateful for the warmth of the fire. She looked over at Chloe, who was doing much the same thing while staring into flames which were popping and crackling now as it dried out the wet wood it was consuming.

They put some turkey and cheese sandwiches wrapped in aluminum foil in amongst some of the new coals to heat up. After they finished eating, Chloe laid on her back and stared up at the sky.

"There's so many of them," she said, looking at the innumerable stars littered across the clear sky.

Sofie looked up, but remained silent.

"He hardly ever gets like this, you know." Chloe got up and moved closer to the fire again.

Sofie looked at her for a moment, then replied, "I know."

"Even in the last few years, ever since... he's still always been there, and... and he's the greatest dad I could hope for." Chloe glanced at Sofie. "I still get to see her occasionally, not right now, but before this... dispute thing, whatever you know. Things were still okay, but now I'm afraid of what will happen, where this will all lead. Why am I even saying all this? It has nothing to do with you. It's just that often I think perhaps there's something I could do, that I could somehow fix this divide between my parents."

Sofie moved closer to Chloe, putting an arm around her shoulders. "We all wish we could just fix the problems that our loved ones get themselves in, but often we can't. This *is* a storm, but all storms pass through eventually. They'll work things out in the end, I'm sure. It just sometimes takes longer than we would like."

"Yes, storms pass," Chloe quietly replied, barely loud enough to hear, "but how much damage will it leave in its wake?"

A little while later, Sofie got to her feet, and in an excited and cheerful tone, said, "Well, I think it's time we finally got to the dessert. I brought fixings for banana boats, and they aren't going to make themselves."

Chloe scrunched up her face as she looked at Sofie. "What in the world is a banana boat?"

Fifteen minutes later, they were pulling the two bundles of tinfoil out of the fire. "I'm still not too sure about this Soph," Chloe said as she pulled back the foil and looked at the melted chocolate and marshmallow stuffed inside of it. Seeing the blackened banana peel, she added, "Perhaps we overcooked them. Mine looks a little burnt."

"It's supposed to be like that. Stop fretting and eat." Sofie handed her a plastic fork. "I always loved these when I had them as a kid."

Chloe took a tentative fork full, looking at it for some time before she put it into her mouth. "it's hot... it's..." she began to say, her mouth still full. She took another bite and finished it before continuing, "It's... well, is it possible for something to be both delicious and disgusting at the same time?"

Sofie laughed, trying not to spit any of the food she had just put into her mouth back out. "I've known certain people not to like it, but I don't think I've heard anyone give it quite that description before."

"The banana tastes burnt and isn't that good, yet it kind of goes with everything at the same time. It's weird. I can't quite make up my mind about it yet."

When Chloe was done, she waded up the tinfoil and threw it into the flames before laying back to look at the sky again. Momentarily, she sprung back upright and was anxiously tugging at Sofie's arm. "Sofie! Sofie, look!" she exclaimed, pointing into the sky.

Startled, Sofie looked to where Chloe was pointing. "Oh wow," she said in awe. Over the lake and extending across the northern horizon was a band of green light which hung in the night sky, gently swaying or rippling as it slowly moved and changed above them.

"The aurora borealis. It's always something when I actually get to see it out there in our sky." There was a sort of reverence in Chloe's voice as she talked.

Sofie's mind went back to when she was a teenager back in Norway, when she and her friends would drive or sometimes even ski out to the middle of nowhere, searching for the northern lights. Sofie lay with her back on the snow and hands behind her head as she watched the green lights dance across the sky, occasionally changing shape and waxing and waning in intensity.

Chloe inched closer to Sofie's side until she was able to rest her head on the crook of Sofie's shoulder. While staring at the sky, she quietly said, "Thank you."

Warmth flooded Sofie's chest when she heard this, feeling that she understood the full weight of those two words in this moment.

Neither of them could ever recall how long it was that they stayed out there like that, watching the lights above before finally turning to the heated tent for sleep.

Sofie continued walking through the woods, ready to do whatever she could to help Chloe. When she again thought about James, anger rose within her once more as she began to hurry along the path, her clothing or pack occasionally getting snagged on a branch, which only increased her agitation. She could sense her pulse rising as the muscles in her legs started to quiver. The light of the flashlight was darting about the trees and the ground when she tripped over an unseen root and fell to the ground.

She stayed there for a moment, feeling the damp coldness of the leaf litter against her cheek, and felt a sudden urge to never get up again. The feeling dissipated, and as she forced herself back up, Sofie took a deep breath, adjusting the pack on her shoulders and brushing some dirt off her jacket. Looking around, she saw that the path had only become narrower, and she could feel the tall pines pressing in around her. "What am I even doing out here? Why am I the only one left to do the right thing? Shit, am I even going the right way? I mean, shouldn't I be getting to this river soon?"

Thinking back once more, Sofie thought on whether she had exaggerated the extent of what the letter from Chloe said. She recalled it again in her head.

After last winter, I count you as a dear friend, and am confident you feel the same. I know what Father is liable to do if this situation doesn't get settled soon. There may be something that I can do about this, though. I am going to see Mother, but I think I could really use your help. I'm already on my way, but if you're willing, meet me at that spot we know. You know, under the borealis.

"I am going to see Mother... I could really use your help... meet me at that spot we know," Sofie reflected out loud. "Don't worry Chloe, I'm coming."

Sofie heard the passive sound of the flowing river before she ever saw it, and as the trail came alongside the riverbank, a sense of relief came to her as she could now be sure she was going the right way. She stooped down, splashing water on her face, and took a brief break before continuing. Her pace was now slow as she maneuvered her way across fallen trees and stump holes, and the occasional alder thicket she had to either squeeze through or go around.

The horizon to the east was getting noticeably lighter, and a new sense of urgency struck Sofie. She knew she must reach Chloe before sunrise, as Gunnar and his people would start to search for her when they found out she was missing. The sooner she found Chloe, the quicker she would understand the extent of the situation she was in and be able to help. She picked up her pace as much as she could, and despite her exhaustion and the fact that she was now falling and getting scraped up by brambles of which she now took little heed of, she was propelled forward by the knowledge that she was the one person that Chloe had asked to help.

The river she had been following fed into a small lake. She thought about how easy and fast this same route had been when she followed it several months prior while on a snowmobile. The shoreline here was open, and Sofie made good speed as she looked over at the eastern horizon where the sun was about to rise. A rock cliff rose fifteen feet along the water's edge, and she knew she was in the right spot. She looked about for some sign, now walking into the woods.

A flickering light beyond several trees caught her attention. A fire! She could see it plainly now as she got closer. It was a small campfire, burning next to a large rock formation, one of the colossal boulders that were scattered across the forest floor. As Sofie approached the campfire, a girl emerged from behind the rock and ran toward her.

Chloe collided with the woman, wrapping her arms around her in a tight embrace. "Sofie! I was starting to wonder if you were actually—I mean, of course I knew you would come. I never had a doubt, really. I knew I could count on you."

"Yes, yes Chloe. I'm here. I'm here now." Sofie managed to say between Chloe's talking. When she pulled herself away from Chloe's embrace, she made her way to the fire and sat down with her back against the stone. "I really am glad to see that you're alright."

"You look exhausted, Sofie. I'm sorry I had to call on your help so suddenly like that, in the middle of the night, I just didn't know who else to turn to for help."

"Of course, of course. It's no problem, I'm happy to help. I'm not sure what I'll be able to do, but there'll be more time to talk about that later. I know we can't stay here. It's already daylight and I'm guessing your dad might look for you here. Just give me five minutes to rest, and I'll be good to continue."

"You go ahead and rest. It's true, we'll have to move on soon, but we can stay for a little while yet. I'll wake you when we need to leave."

"Just need five minutes, that's all. Then we need to keep moving." Sofie was already closing her eyes.

CHAPTER 11

James was running as fast as he dared to within the dark and dense woods. Small trees crowded close together and prohibited him from moving as quickly as he would have liked. Even with this caution, he tripped over a fallen tree, quickly getting back up and running just as fast as before. The beam of light from his flashlight danced haphazardly about the thin branches and leaves damp with dew that kept whipping him in the face, and the roots and logs that were strewn across the ground as if they were placed there for the sole reason to trip him up. He paused, listening for any sound of someone else nearby, but only heard a nearby owl hooting. He gauged what would be his best path through the forest, before running again, only occasionally stumbling over a rock or woody debris.

"Chloe!" James felt strange yelling out her name. After all, she didn't know him. What might she be thinking right now, having some stranger chasing after her like this? How could she trust him, and why should she stop and let him talk to her? "Chloe, I'm with Sofie! I'm here to help!" *I'm here to help? That's a stupid thing to say, isn't it?*

James stopped running, resting his hand against a tree. "What am I even doing, anyway?" *What would I even do if I did find her? And regardless, I'm not going to find her in this forest and darkness. Well, I tried. I just need to find my way back and onto the road again, then I can leave this whole ridiculous mess behind.*

James turned around, facing the direction he had come in, and started walking. He was careful now to stay to a straight course back as he walked through dense thickets of saplings and clambering over fallen trees. The sound of high-pitched yipping and howling of coyotes began somewhere in the distance.

He should have found the road by now, but with the trees spaced close together and the thick brush about, it was difficult to keep a straight path. He remembered that he had always kept a compass in his backpack, and now he searched through the contents. With his flashlight in hand, he looked over every pocket two, and even three times, but he couldn't find any compass. Somewhere in the course of unpacking and repacking, he must have taken it out and never put it back in. He looked up to the night sky but could only see small patches of stars through the dense canopy, and wasn't able to locate Polaris, the North Star. He kept pushing forward, trying to force all other thoughts from his mind other than staying on the same course the best he could. He came to an opening where there was a sparse tree canopy, and gazing at the sky, he located the North Star. This only helped him a little, as he had no idea what direction he ran in when he entered the woods, and he realized he may not have even stayed on a straight path running mindlessly in the dark. He now knew, however, that the current direction he was walking was due east, but he had no way of knowing whether this would lead back to the road.

After several more minutes, James stopped and collapsed to the ground with his back against the large trunk of a standing tree. He couldn't seem to stop the slight trembling in his limbs, and his breath was coming out shaky and uneven as the full weight of his current situation set in on him.

Not only was there the fact that he should have stumbled onto the road a while ago if he was headed in the right direction, but also the forest structure here differed from what he had run through on his way in. There were broad towering pines which made up a sparse canopy, with a dense mixture of pine and hardwood saplings six to fifteen feet tall underneath, making running almost impossible. This compared to the more evenly spaced mid-sized trees of predominantly hardwoods, which he had initially run through. He had either been walking in the wrong direction the whole time or he had deviated from the intended direction somewhere along the way.

It took all his willpower to keep the fear from wrapping itself about him, and leading his mind along dark avenues of thought, but he managed to push it back. He unslung his backpack from off his shoulders, unzipping it at his feet. With the flashlight in hand, he searched through the contents of the bag. The backpack was packed and used for smaller hikes, for whenever he would come to an area or trail whilst on the road where he could get out for what was usually only a short hike.

He took a mental inventory as he went through. One 20-ounce bottle of water, a light waterproof jacket, one half-empty bag of beef jerky, one quarter full bag of trail mix, two granola bars, one survival knife with a 5 in. blade, one Leatherman multi-tool, a set of ear buds, one cigar, and one lighter.

James decided there was no point in trying to walk anywhere tonight and that it was best to wait for daylight before deciding on what to do. His first plan of action was to make a fire. So, James walked a little further yet, finding a more open area without saplings where the immense pine trees were far apart, and the ground was mainly dirt and pine needles.

He built up a small pile of various tinder—paper birch bark, dry moss, and dead pine needles. On top of that, he laid the kindling—mostly just twigs and small branches—and then larger branches and logs were set nearby as well. Luckily, it appeared to not have rained recently, and everything was fairly dry. Pulling the lighter out of his backpack, he tried lighting the thinnest section of bark, and on his second attempt it lit up, the fire slowly spreading to the rest of the tinder, and soon there was a good flame going.

James had gathered more wood and now had plenty to last throughout the night. He put on the jacket that was in the pack, feeling the chill in the night air, and sat quite close to the fire, gazing into the flames as he thought about Elena and the time he spent with her. A wolf howled in the distance, which was quickly followed by several more howls. The croaking of frogs and other sounds of wildlife suddenly seemed to become more acute.

After some time, the sky began to lighten and James laid down next to the freshly stoked fire, using his backpack as a pillow, trying to get as comfortable as he could on the hard ground. He tried for what seemed like a long time to fall asleep without success. Birds began to chirp and sing above him, and he couldn't help but think that every rustle of the leaves could be a bear, when most likely it was nothing more than a squirrel or chipmunk.

CHAPTER 12

"...Sofie, Sofie, I'm sorry, but we have to leave now." Chloe was gently shaking Sofie's shoulder until she finally stirred.

Sofie stared bleary-eyed at the girl standing over her. After a moment and without saying a word, she got up and slowly slung her heavy pack over her shoulders and stood waiting for the girl to lead.

"Don't worry, we won't have to travel far today," Chloe said as she started walking. "I know a place where we can rest without fear of being found."

They had been walking for a little while when Sofie noticed how high the sun was in the sky. "How long did you let me sleep? I said I only needed a brief rest; I didn't even mean to fall asleep."

"As long as I could reasonably allow. Don't worry though, Sofie," Chloe quickly added, "Father probably won't even spend much time looking for me. He knows where I'm going... and it's there where he will now go. The pieces are finally moving." Chloe paused in her stride, looking back at Sofie briefly before continuing again. "We will finally see a resolution this time... at least of some sort."

"You did leave your dad a note, then?" Sofie cautiously asked.

"I did."

They walked in silence now, and Sofie tried not to think about the ache in her legs. Her whole body seemed to go stiff while she had slept, and now it took all she had just to keep up with the girl in front of her. She lost all track of time as she continued onward, barely even thinking as they pressed on. She almost collided with Chloe when she abruptly halted in front of a dense thicket of spruce trees.

The girl half turned toward Sofie. "Follow me," she said and pushed through the densely grown spruce.

Chloe had almost disappeared in the foliage before Sofie followed. She pushed her way through the branches of many densely grown saplings and was about to ask why they couldn't find a way around this mess when she stumbled into a clearing. She looked around at what they were now standing in, her eyes widening. They were in a circular clearing of moss and needle litter on the ground about thirty feet in diameter and encircled by a dense wall of spruce encompassing them.

"This is... I mean, how did you ever find this?" Sofie asked, still looking around at her surroundings.

"There used to be a little deer trail leading into here, and I guess I just stumbled into it one day when I was wondering around. I come here now and then, mostly when I just need to get away. It's funny, when I find myself within these green walls, I feel both free and safe. Once, me and a friend snuck out here one night, and we just laid on the ground and stared at the stars." Chloe looked up into the sky, as if lost in thought. "Well, anyway, we can stay here and rest. Nobody is going to find us."

After sitting down to rest, Sofie finally ventured to ask the question which had been on her mind since she first read that note. "So, Chloe, you know I have to ask, what is it that you plan on doing exactly?"

Chloe gave her a weary smile. "Despite whatever my dad or mom may say is the reason for this dispute, I know the truth. They will say it's about a land dispute or over timber rights, but I know that's not true, not really, not at the core. No, it's about me."

"Chloe, that's not true—"

"But it is! This all only started when my mom left. And ever since then, I've been at the center of all of it. The questions of who I'm going to stay with, the blame of who's at fault, the talk behind closed doors that no one thinks I hear, but I do. All this hostility only really began when my parents split up, and now these two groups of differing people led on either side by each of my parents are about to go to war with each other. This is all between my father and mother, and who's at the center of that, it's me, their only child! All of this is because of me."

"That's not true. This is about much more than what happened between your parents. Even if it was, it has nothing to do with you, you're just unfortunately caught up in the middle of it." Sofie walked closer to Chloe so that she could look her more in the eyes. "Now you listen to me. None of this is your fault. You're not to blame for any of it, okay? Come here." Sofie hugged her.

"It doesn't matter if I'm not to blame, I'm still in the middle of it," Chloe said while still being held in the other woman's embrace. "And I find myself in a position where maybe I can bring it all to a conclusion."

Sofie released the girl and took a step back. "And how do you propose to do this?"

"Since you were last here, things have only gotten more tense, and I have been forbidden from seeing Mother. Simply by going to her will bring them both to an actual personal confrontation. That's the first step, and then with your help as someone who is mostly a neutral party, we can talk to both of them and hopefully bring all of this to a peaceful conclusion."

"Well, I'm not sure how much that will accomplish or not, but perhaps you're right and it will be enough.

Either way, I will do all I can to help you in bringing about a resolution to this."

Chloe briefly hugged Sofie again and thanked her, then she sat down next to her own pack. After a little while she ventured to say, "You know, when you were here before, when everything was happening back at the house and you took me out to the lake, and there was all that snow and ice?"

"Yes."

"I never said thank you."

"And you never had to."

"No, I mean... it's just, you seemed to be there when I needed it most. And well, you made me feel like a kid again."

Sofie smiled, then she reclined with her head propped up on the pack and soon fell asleep.

She woke up as the sun was waning on the western horizon. She didn't have a tent in her pack, but seeing that the sky still looked clear, she was happy to sleep under the stars with just her sleeping bag and tarp. Together, they cooked up some freeze-dried food for dinner over a camp stove Sofie had brought and they talked. She felt a sense of comfort in being able to just sit there with Chloe, surrounded by the trees, laughing and reminiscing, almost seeming to forget their current circumstance.

CHAPTER 13

When the sun had risen above the treetops, James felt like he hadn't slept at all, but he must have been drifting in and out of sleep intermittently, because hours had passed by, and it was now late morning. He thought about starting the campfire back up again, but figured there wasn't any point. He decided that his best option was to choose a direction and walk as straight a course as he could manage without a compass. His food and water supply were very limited, and he would have to cover as much ground as he could early on, hoping to find some sign of civilization somewhere. He started looking about on the ground nearby and picked up a small rock which was roughly arrow shaped. Placing this rock on a bare spot of exposed soil, he spun it with his hand. The direction the rock pointed was mostly north, judging by the position of the rising sun. Slowly getting to his feet, James slid the backpack over his shoulders and walked in the direction given by the rock, knowing that he was likely only heading further into the heart of the wilderness

The sun was still high in the sky, as it filtered down through the predominantly pine and spruce canopy to where James sat. He looked at the water bottle, which was more than half empty already, and it was likely only mid-afternoon. So much for conserving his resources for as long as he could. The food looked a little better, as only now did he allow himself to eat a little of the trail mix he had. His feet ached, and there was a heavy soreness throughout almost every major muscle in his legs. James had convinced himself that he was only going deeper into the forest and away from civilization, as he had feared he might, but this conclusion didn't alter his course of action.

Looking back up at the sky, James knew he needed to get up and continue trudging through these woods. Getting to his feet and feeling the renewed pain and stiffness from sitting shoot through his legs, he continued forward. He thought about how far he needed to travel yet that day and questioned whether he should follow prominent terrain features like a ridgeline. He wanted to find some high point where he could look out and scan the surrounding landscape for any point of interest, but currently, the topography remained relatively flat. He had almost walked right by when he noticed a small patch of wild leeks. Dropping to his knees, he greedily began to pluck them out of the soil, eating leaf and bulb. He harvested every plant he saw in the small patch, putting several in his backpack for later eating before continuing on.

He wasn't sure when he first noticed the constant hum that was in the air, but now he recognized the sound and quickened his pace. James broke through a cedar thicket and came abruptly to the cause of the noise. He stood upon the bank of a river about thirty feet wide, where the roar of the rushing water continually moved past him.

James dropped his pack and rushed to the edge of the water, dipping his hand in, and feeling the refreshing chill rush against his skin. The water looked clear, and after drinking what little he had left, James filled his bottle from the stream. He thought about what he could do to purify the water before drinking it. Boiling came to mind, but then James remembered he didn't have any pots or containers that he could boil it in. The water appeared clean as James looked at the liquid inside his bottle, so he drank his fill, the water tasting clean, cold, and refreshing, filling the bottle a second time.

He decided to follow the river downstream, and this way he would maintain a water supply, as well as providing a sure route, instead of just wandering about aimlessly. After resting on the riverbank for a little while, watching the water rush by, James got up and, turning downstream he continued his hike once more.

Several hours later, the sun was low on the horizon and the light was dimming in the forest. James made camp beneath a few cedar trees close to the bank of the river. He made a fire, eating his last granola bar and half of the beef jerky that was left. It seemed to do little to satiate his hunger, but he felt like he ate more than he probably should have, and he tried to focus on the thought of finding a road or some form of civilization as he stared at the fire. When he laid down, he realized how truly exhausted he was and found sleep relatively quickly.

CHAPTER 14

The next morning, Sofie was getting her stuff together to leave when Chloe finally woke up. "I made some coffee, if you want any. I don't know if you drink that or not."

"I'll take a little, thanks," Chloe said as she yawned. "I guess I must've overslept."

"Not at all. Take your time. I remember crossing a stream shortly before entering this little spot. I'm going to go and fill up our water bottles."

"I can go with you. Just give me a minute."

"No need, it isn't far. And I think I can find my way there and back easy enough."

"Well, okay. You know, I'm quite excited to see my mom again today."

"Of course you are. Be back in a minute."

Sofie felt better than the day before, but she still had a deep apprehension about the way things might turn out in the end. The sky was clear and blue above her, and as she was walking and listening to the birds in the trees, she thought she heard something off to her right—the sound of snapping twigs and rustling of leaves—like someone else was out here besides just her. Sofie stopped a moment, listening. A sense of sudden foreboding passed through her mind like a shadow. She didn't hear the sound again, so she discarded this feeling and moved on. She briefly continued forward before hearing the same noise as before and stopped once more. A snap of twigs and rustle of leaves, and then again, the sound continued, and it was louder now. Someone—or something—was definitely nearby.

A bear suddenly emerged from behind some trees. It shook its head, and then bared its teeth in a low growl. It took a few more steps, the long dark brown fur rustling on the hump above its shoulders, and then stopped, standing about ten yards from where Sofie stood. She froze, standing rigid as tremors ran through her whole body. There was a sound of leaves crunching behind her and she turned her head to look. Standing not far behind her was a bear cub, looking at her with an inquisitive curiosity. Sofie looked forward again at the grizzly bear sow, who was now opening its enormous jaw and letting out several deep, guttural roars.

"Oh, fuck." Sofie hardly had a second to think of what she could do before the grizzly broke into a sprint, ramming right into her. The impact threw her to the side, lifting her off her feet before she landed hard on her back. Before she could try to struggle back to her feet, she felt the bear's massive jaw clamp down hard onto her upper thigh, teeth tearing through flesh. Sofie screamed, shrill and loud, as intense pain overwhelmed her. A moment later she was being swung back and forth, dragged through the leaves and bramble of the ground like a rag doll, the bear's jaw remaining clamped onto her thigh. Then her leg was released, and she was thrown in the air, landing several feet away and rolling onto her stomach.

She groaned and was trying to decide whether to try and fight back or play dead. A pocketknife was the only weapon she had at her disposal, and she was still trying to decide what to do when she felt one of its massive paws on her back. The weight pressing down on her was unbearable, and she struggled to breathe with her lungs being compressed against the ground. She could hear it now, its nostrils sniffing right above her head, its muzzle pressing into the hair at the back of her head. Sofie didn't move, tried not to make a sound, not to even breathe. After a moment, it seemed like the bear had lifted its head back and away from her, but still the paw remained, pinning her to the earth.

Suddenly—unexpectedly—Sofie felt its teeth again, this time tearing through the flesh around her right shoulder. She screamed again, even louder than the first time, as if that were possible. It felt like the bear had come up with half her shoulder as its jaw tore away from her. The claws of the paw that had her pinned down suddenly dug deeply into her back—she screamed again. The bear started to push her forward against the ground, and then backwards again, all with that one paw which was now dug into her back.

Abruptly, the claws released from her skin, and the weight upon her back was gone. She didn't know what that meant, but tried to play dead. The bear forcefully turned her over onto her back with its head, and in a moment, both front paws were now pressed on top of her torso, and she stared into its yellow eyes. Sofie couldn't do anything, submitting to whatever fate this powerful creature had in store for her. It took all her strength just to say what she was about to say. She meant to scream it out at this creature, but with the tremendous weight upon her stomach and chest, it only came out as a whisper.

"Well... if you're going to do it, do it then. Let's finish this—kill me. Kill me now if you're gonna do it."

Sofie was barely aware of the sound that started to vibrate through the ground, and the shouting that she became faintly aware of seemed to be only a hallucination. The bear turned its head, as if it was looking at something else. She was becoming dizzy and seemed to be losing consciousness, not sure what was real or only a trick of her mind, but there was no mistaking that in a moment the weight was gone, the bear was absent. She wasn't sure what was happening, but there seemed to be a great commotion around her, with a thudding chorus sounding upon the ground, like a significant trampling of feet around the dirt nearby. An image came into her head—that of horses, wild horses. A great horde of wild horses dashing off together across a vast green field. Black, white, spotted, brown— all running, all free. There didn't seem to be any pain anymore.

Chloe was brewing more coffee when she heard the scream pass along in the wind. She wasn't even fully aware of what she was hearing. It seemed like the wind itself took on a voice as it shrieked across the sky. Her face became ashen as she realized what she was hearing, but she was frozen in place, feeling her pulse beat beneath the skin. She heard it again, the unmistakable sound of a scream, however distant. *Sofie!* Without a moment's more hesitation, Chloe sprinted into the forest toward the faint scream.

There were six riders on horseback galloping swiftly through the woods. They were yelling, as if they were charging into battle. The lead rider had a long spear held out straight ahead of him.

The grizzly bear, which was standing on top of a woman, looked over toward them as they approached. The sound of yelling intensified as the lead rider adjusted the spear against his shoulder.

The spearhead entered just where the rider intended, right behind its front shoulder. The shaft of the spear shattered after the spearhead sank deeply into fat and muscle, and the rider was flung from the horse and fell hard to the ground, as the bear toppled over off the woman and onto its side. Two of the riders got off their horses and knelt by the woman as the other riders circled around them. Some of them gathered around the grizzly, who was struggling to get back up, the broken spear sticking out from its side. One rider had a bow and shot an arrow which sunk deep into its skull, while another rider had a spear and drove it with all his strength into the grizzly's chest. While this was happening, one rider had dismounted and was kneeling in front of the bear's head, murmuring to it and stroking its head as it struggled to take its last few breaths of life.

"She's still alive," stated a woman who was gathering bandages and dressings from a saddlebag.

"Yes, but she appears to be fading," said Molteeb, the man who first struck the bear, as he was now kneeling by Sofie's head, checking vitals. "Hurry, Shanni, we must be quick if we hope to save her."

"Aye Molteeb, so it's not too late—please let us not be too late." Shanni knelt at Sofie's side with her supplies. She looked at the mauled and mutilated leg. "She's sure had her way with this one, hasn't she?" Shanni looked over to where the great bear was lying, and then back at Sofie. "Poor soul," she said as she got to work, trying to patch up the leg as best she could.

Chloe burst into the clearing, shaking uncontrollably. With rapid blinking, her gaze darted about, trying to take in the scene in front of her. A huge brown bear laying on the ground, a cub cautiously walking up to it. People were scurrying about, dressed in furs and leathers, two of whom were kneeling near the bear—

"Sofie!" Chloe screamed as soon as she saw the body that they were kneeling next to. She ran toward her as fast as she could.

"Someone grab that girl!" Shanni yelled, as she continued to bandage Sofie's wounds after momentarily glancing at the hysterical girl who was running toward them.

Ishti, who was the closest, saw the girl and hastened to intercept her. He ran into her path and grabbed Chloe before she reached the body, her momentum pulling them both to the ground.

"Sofie! Tell me she's not dead," Chloe yelled as she struggled with the man holding her down. "Let me see her, I have to see, to know. Let me go."

"Whoa, be still, little bird. We are doing all we can."

The other three riders now came over to where Sofie lay, the bear being taken care of. "Molteeb?" asked one of them, addressing the man kneeling at Sofie's head.

"Her wounds are deep; we need to get her back to the village as quickly as possible. You know what to do," Molteeb said to the three gathered around.

The three conversed with each other for a moment and then went to work, one going to the saddlebags, while the other two searched through the nearby fallen branches.

Molteeb was wrapping some of Sofie's lesser injuries, and looking over to see how Shanni was managing, "We need to stop the bleeding if she's going to survive the trip back. She's already lost a lot of blood."

"I'm doing all I... you think you can do better, that sow sure took a good bit of flesh along with her when she let go of the leg. There's a lot of missing skin here. It's difficult without proper supplies." Shanni wiped sweat from her forehead and then started wrapping thin cloth around the makeshift bandage as tightly as she could.

Chloe became still, and her breathing slowed as she focused on the two individuals kneeling next to the body, and saw that they were bandaging her up, helping her. "Okay, okay, I get it. Can I just go to her? I need to see that she's not..."

"She's not. You need to let us help her though," Ishti said, as he continued to sit with the girl and hold her back. "The bear attacked her, and we just got here ourselves. We're going to have to bring her back to our village. We'll do everything we can for her."

"Well, can you at least let me get up? I can help."

The other three people came over, carrying a crude stretcher, and laid it down next to the woman. Ishti let Chloe get to her feet, but still held onto her.

Molteeb exchanged a few words with the men that arrived with the stretcher and got up to his feet, looking over at the girl. His gaze froze for a moment in recognition when he met Chloe's eyes. He walked over to her, and kneeling, placed both hands on either shoulder, looking into her eyes. "The woman is alive, though gravely injured, and we must get her to our healer as soon as possible. You're Chloe, aren't you? Your mother will be thrilled to see you."

Not five minutes later, they were on the move. Sofie was lying on the makeshift stretcher, framed out by straight branches which were tied together as a rectangular frame with a thick blanket stretched and tied off between it. They then tied Sofie down to the stretcher as well for support. Shanni led the way with Chloe by her side looking for the clearest path ahead as Molteeb and Ishti carried Sofie and were practically running as they hurried through the forest, all the while keeping the stretcher between them incredibly still as they appeared to glide across the forest floor. The other three that were with them stayed behind to skin and process the bear before heading back.

CHAPTER 15

In the morning, James had made another fire, being in no rush to start another day of mindless walking. There was also a chill in the morning air, and James was grateful for a bit of warmth. He had slept through the night, only waking up two or three times and falling right back to sleep, and now, even though he was still sore, he felt well rested, despite sleeping on the hard ground.

James put the fire out, spreading the coals apart and mixing them in the dirt. He got up and was about to put his backpack on when he glanced toward the river—something caught his attention. It was only a brief glimpse before it disappeared behind the brush, but he could have sworn it looked like a person. He gazed in that direction, and a little while later, he saw it again. A glimpse of clothing, of hair, as the figure moved through the trees, disappearing, and then reappearing through a gap in the woods. The figure paused in one of these sparse openings, turning toward him, then quickly disappearing again.

No, it can't be. "Hello?" James called out, still not sure what he was seeing, and equally unsure of what to say. "Wait… just…" slinging his pack on, he started running toward where the figure had disappeared.

As he ran, any stiffness he had felt just a moment ago was gone, rushing toward where the figure had disappeared.

There was nothing. James stopped to catch his breath, the sound of the flowing water off to his left now barely audible. He didn't want to lose his way again, so he walked back to the riverbank and continued alongside it. He already doubted what he had thought he saw, attributing it to exhaustion and mild delirium.

James stopped for a brief water break. When looking back up, he saw a person crouched down by the riverside. The figure was more than a hundred feet away, but this time in clear view. The person stood up and looked toward him, and he was sure that the individual was a woman. She turned and started walking away, disappearing beyond a bend in the river. James was motionless, staring out as she vanished from view. *It's not her, it can't be.* "Hey there, hold up," he finally called out. He didn't run, but continued on at a steady pace, figuring that he must be imagining things, though still unsure.

A gust of wind blew through the trees, and James thought he heard a faint whisper of a scream drift by. A deep sense of sorrow which he didn't understand passed over him, like a voice from very far away was calling out to him. He stood still for a long moment, looking out toward the wind, but heard nothing else.

Around noon James took a break, sitting against the bole of a large tree. Hunger was gnawing at his gut, but he refrained from eating, trying to ration out what little he had left. He drank his fill of water and got up once more to continue forward. Glancing back along the river, he saw her again.

She was standing on the riverbank only about twenty feet away. Her back was to him as she was looking out across the river, then she turned toward him.

His mind flashed back to a memory on the Alaskan coastline when he saw her looking back at him like this, that faint smile on her lips showing a genuine happiness while her eyes were filled with sadness, her blonde hair blowing in the breeze. And now here she was again, standing by a water's edge, looking just the same, even wearing the same orange long-sleeve shirt and jeans he had first saw her in. James stood staring at Elena, not daring to look away for even the briefest moment for fear that this visage might vanish. How long this moment lasted, James could never recall later. It might have been for only the briefest of seconds or it could have lasted for several minutes, he could never say. He only knew that he had stood there, letting the beauty of that moment wash over him, not caring or thinking of what reason could have brought about this moment.

Elena walked toward him. She stopped, being within a few feet from him, and said, "You need to get moving James, many miles are to be covered yet. There is still time left."

James grabbed his pack, looking down for only a second, and when he looked back up, she was gone. He looked about the area, but there wasn't any sign of her. James started walking, continuing his route along the river as he consciously decided there wasn't anything at all strange about what had just happened, or what the state of his mind was in to conjure up the realistic imaginings of a dead woman. The sound of her voice echoed in his head, that seductive way in which she spoke his name, bringing back a rush of memories. He replayed the encounter through his head, dissecting the movements that she had made, the words she said, and what they might mean.

The river made its way in wide, sweeping curves as it snaked its way through the broad valley. James continued through the day at a moderately slow but steady pace. The walking didn't bother him much as his mind was occupied with other thoughts, most of which being directly related to Elena. Beyond simply hoping and looking forward to any more subsequent visions of this woman, he also began to replay every moment and memory he had experienced with her in his head. And even though it hurt to think about, hurt to remember and replay and fantasize about what could be if she was still alive, there was a fascination to it, a morbid sense of satisfaction in reliving a time and memory that was dead. Yes, it hurt, it hurt deep within his very being, but the memories were real, and they were a part of him now, a part that he would never want to forget no matter how much despair they held. And through dwelling on this, these memories, this woman that he could not possibly help but think about, the time that he had spent with her; it all became even more beautiful than it actually was in real life. Such is the way with memory, distorting the landscape of the past, editing out the parts that would inhibit a moment from becoming the beautiful memory that it eventually becomes with time. James knew that his mind was already doing this, and didn't care, because he would rather spend every moment while wandering in these woods dwelling on the memory of Elena—the good memories—and even imagine that she was still here walking along with him, instead of thinking about the hopeless predicament he was in.

As the day drew toward evening, James stumbled through the woods, even falling a few times as he tripped over a rock or a log. Not giving much heed any longer, even to the mosquitos that had continued to pester him almost nonstop. He hardly paid attention to anything that was outside of the world in which he was living in within his own mind. All the many moments he had had with Elena continuing to play and replay through his head. Of the first time he had seen her, Elena's still unconscious body lying on the shore after he had dragged her from the water. How she would stand at the water's edge and stare across the bay and into the mountainous horizon. Of her slowly dancing in front of the fireplace. The sound of her laugh. The sadness in her eyes. The touch of her skin. The weight of her lips on his. A horrified look upon her face. Elena huddled in the corner of a room weeping. That look she had on her face in the dark woods before reaching Cole's house, the raw pleading of her voice. That knife clenched in her hand. How she held the blade, trembling against her skin. Her voice, "Don't forget about me, James." That slow continuous motion of the blade across her throat as it cut deeply—and... the blood—flowing down.

James fell to the ground, weeping, surrendering to the emotions he was feeling.

At some point, he heard a voice saying, "Get up. Get up, James." When he looked up, Elena was there, standing next to him. She reached out her hand toward him.

James grabbed her hand and was pulled to his feet. As he looked at her, he asked, "Is this a dream?"

"If this is a dream, then let it be a beautiful dream," she answered.

James couldn't help himself from further asking, "but... could it be real?"

"What is reality but our own perceptions? And who's would this be then? My reality, your reality, or the way things really are?"

"But how are we to know... the way things really are?"

Elena laughed, "I think we're both well beyond worrying about that. Now come, we need to find a place to make camp." She was then off, walking out ahead at a brisk pace.

"We?" James asked himself as he followed behind her. It wasn't long before she had stopped again, leaning against a tree now. Next to where she stood was a flat open area, where several slabs of rock laid out along the river's edge with a thin layer of dirt and moss over sections of it. James dropped his pack in this small clearing, taking another lingering glance at Elena, who had her back toward him looking out along the river. He walked away to gather firewood before it got dark.

When James got back from carrying several armloads of dead limbs and other wood scattered across the nearby forest floor, Elena was nowhere to be seen. He soon had a fire going and sat with his back against a tree, looking toward the fire and the darkening sky above the trees. Hunger struck him again like a deepening pit growing within his gut, and he thought about the genuine possibility of dying in these woods. Settling into a somewhat comfortable position, he felt a light and cool breeze and heard the soft crackle of the fire giving off just the right amount of heat. As this sound combined with the constant hum of the river, it provided a sense of comfort and ease rather than that of apprehension or fear. *Perhaps it's not so bad, this.*

"Waiting for the end?"

James jumped a little as he heard Elena's voice. He looked over and saw her sitting against a nearby tree, staring up at the sky.

"No, it's not so bad, easing away," she continued. "Finding a place to rest and letting the leaves drift over you like a quilt, to wait until the snow covers you up." Elena looked straight at him, "It's okay, James, you can follow me into those shadows."

James found something comforting in the way she said these words. Then images flashed through his mind again—a blood stain expanding through clothing—

dripping onto the ground—a blank stare, lifeless. "No!" James sprung to his feet. "You know I can't, I won't. Even if I wanted to, I couldn't do that now, not anymore. Not at least until my debt to you is paid."

"You owe me nothing. There is no debt."

"Of course there is. The moment you took your life, you indebted me to you. You bought my life with yours. If I were to die now, it would make your sacrifice meaningless."

"James, your life has always been yours, to live or waste as you choose. None of that has changed. Just as my life had always been mine, and the choices I made led me to the conclusion of it. My death likewise is my own, it is not yours to claim or be beholden to."

"Yes, it was your choice, your decision. But I was the one who failed you, the one who led you back to his house, into his hands, and in the last moment when I had one more chance to save you, to absolve myself of my failures, I wasn't able to. In the end, I was left there alive, with nothing but loss and emptiness, standing in that darkness with only an unspoken oath remaining."

"You speak as if everything revolves around you." Elena stepped closer toward James. "Think back and look at it logically to see the truth. It was me who came to you, me who deceived you and lied to you. Me who brought you into Cole's games. I am the one responsible for getting you into all of it. And when that final moment came, I wasn't going to let you take the fall, not after everything I did to get us there. It was always going to be me. It had to be me in the end, because it was my fate, not yours."

James looked at her for a long moment before finally saying, "Did I really mean so little to you then, to have no effect on your decision?"

Elena took another slow step forward to where they were now only about a foot apart from each other. "Oh James, don't you understand? It was only because you meant everything in that moment that I did what I did. It was my choice, my fate. There is no debt, no unspoken oath."

As James looked at her, so close to him now, that sad yet comforting look upon her face, the gentle breeze rustling through her hair, he realized he was looking upon a memory and not a real face. "But... but of course you're not even real. So what does any of this even matter?"

"I'm real to you."

"Are you... I don't think I can be trusted to answer that anymore."

"I'm standing here, aren't I?"

"But you're dead."

"Why does that have to matter?"

"Because... you're not really you, are you? You're..."

Elena moved her open hand up to James's cheek, letting it hover inches away from contact. "I'm what? I'm you? A figment of your imagination? Perhaps I'm what you need me to be right now."

"But you're not really her then? No, of course you're not."

"You're tired, James. Go to sleep. Everything will be better in the morning."

James realized that indeed he was exhausted. It wasn't long after James laid down next to the fire that he was fast asleep.

CHAPTER 16

James had walked a good five miles before midday, and now took a long rest, being exhausted. He started on his way soon after waking up, not bothering with a fire, and not wanting to sit with his thoughts for too long. He was relieved and maybe also a little saddened that there was no sign of Elena that morning, and he couldn't help but wonder if she was gone for good or not.

The river continued its winding path, sometimes through narrow valleys, forcing James to climb up along the top of a bluff and follow its ridgeline for a while until the landscape on the river's edge flatted out once more. Many small tributaries joined the river from time to time, but it continued its course much the same as it had.

He walked on and on with a renewed purpose, traveling more miles now than any previous day, and this, with his continued hunger and the aches and soreness in what seemed to extend throughout his entire body. He pushed himself on, trying not to think about why or to what purpose he did this, only that he continued to move. Continuing to follow the river, the day had waned into late afternoon, and James was filling up his water bottle again and taking another break when he heard a familiar voice.

"Where are you going?" Elena asked, leaning against a nearby tree. "What are you hoping to find?"

"You know, wherever this river eventually leads—"

"You know what I mean. Stop running James."

"I'm trying to sur—"

"Find the girl. Find them both and help them."

James stared at her for a moment. "It's not my problem."

"If that was true, then why did Sofie ask for your help? What impulse made you run into the forest after Chloe? Find the girl, James." Elena stood up from the tree she was leaning against and started walking ahead of him. "Now let's go. We have a long way to travel yet."

James had no idea how many miles he had walked since Elena had returned. He only knew that she now remained there, always ahead of him, always too far away to converse with, but still within sight.

"Elena, we must make camp. It's getting too dark," James yelled. She paused now, and James was able to catch up to her.

"Not yet, we must press on, there is time yet in the day."

"But it's fast getting dark. I can already hardly see what's in front of me. There will be plenty of time tomorrow where we can once again see where we're going. I'm exhausted. Surely we've put on enough miles for one day?"

"You have a flashlight in your bag. Use it. We must continue, come on," Elena said as she was already moving ahead of him again.

"Okay, this is getting ridiculous. What am I even doing?" James asked himself, but he was already getting out his flashlight and taking a swig of water. He was aware of the absurdity of the situation, that he was being led in the dark by a ghost, a figment of his imagination, some externalization of his subconscious. But she seemed so visceral, so real, and he felt compelled to continue to follow, to not lose sight of her, to push on at whatever cost.

It was night; the sky was dark, and to make matters worse, it had started to rain. Still, James continued after Elena, now relying fully on his flashlight. His progress was slower now as he had to watch his footing more carefully, but when he would shine his light ahead, he could always find Elena not too far in the distance. He was wet, cold, and exhausted to the point of collapsing, yet he had mostly become numb to his aches and pains and his movements became mindless and robotic at this point. He wouldn't allow himself to stop, not while that woman remained always in front of him, wordlessly pulling him forward. He thought about whether he would be able to get a fire started in this rain, about the prospect of laying in the cold wet dirt and trying to sleep without shelter in the rain. Pushing these thoughts back, he mindlessly trudged on.

He had lost track of time when his light flitted across Elena, and he saw that she was standing still. He stopped as well when he caught up to her, catching his breath and drinking some water. The rain was steady and unrelenting, and the ground was already getting muddy in some places. His pants were soaked through, and the rain was even seeping through his rain jacket now. James looked at Elena and saw that she was staring out across the river, which remained just off to their left. Following her gaze, James saw something. Moving a little closer and peering between the trees, he saw a light out across the river—two distinct glows of light right next to each other. He became aware that he was peering upon the face of a dwelling, a human dwelling, a small cabin of some sort. The glow he was seeing was emanating from two windows, doubtless the product of a fire from inside. He couldn't believe his eyes and thought that he had to be imagining it. He shined his light around looking for Elena, but he couldn't see her anywhere. The cabin was still there when he looked back. He started to believe that this must be real and knew that he had to make his way to this dwelling.

Wading across the river was challenging, being that it was dark, and he couldn't see his footing. He had debated briefly whether he should try to find a better place to cross, but he could see little in the dark, regardless. Cautiously, he made a few steps into the water, letting the initial shock of the cold pass through him, and continued his way slowly, feeling his way with his feet. He feared it may be deeper than he had originally thought, but the water only came up to his hips at the deepest part, and before he knew it, he was across to the other side.

CHAPTER 17

Nestled within the undergrowth and trees as if it was a part of these woods, sat a small wood cabin with a soft, warm glow emanating from its two front windows. The glow of a fire within gave it a comforting appearance, but the way the cabin sat low to the ground, almost as if it was sinking into the soil, it stood there like a threatening presence as well in the night surrounded by shadowy trees. There was a rudimentary feeling to it of being entirely built by hand, not to say that it wasn't well constructed.

It struck James momentarily that it looked like what he would imagine a witch's abode to look like from some fairytale, especially nestled deep within the forest like this. An image flickered across his mind of a stereotypical old woman huddled over a caldron boiling potions or whatever else. Smoke was drifting out of the cobblestone chimney, and James shook that image away as being ridiculous. He wasn't able to keep his heartbeat from racing, however, at the notion of knocking at that door and seeking admittance. He was gripping onto a nearby tree branch so tightly that his knuckles started to turn white as he thought, *Who would answer on the other side?*

The rain seemed to increase, and he was freezing in his wet clothing, feeling the temperature continuing to drop. Despite his fear, he already knew that he was going to knock on that door.

James walked up to the cabin feeling as cold and wet as ever, his feet swishing in the water of his shoes, but as he stood in front of the door, he hesitated. *Anyone living out here can't appreciate some stranger knocking on his door in the middle of the night. But what choice do I have?* Suppressing gruesome images coming into his head, he lifted his hand, and with a fist, gave three hard knocks to the solid wood. He waited a moment. Nothing. He raised his fist again—the door opened with a creak part way. A face peered through the opening of the door. It was an older rough face with a long, mostly gray beard flowing messily down to his stomach. The gray hair on his head coming down on either side of his face in an unkept manner. Brown eyes shone forth from his face with a searching kind of intensity, but they were also soft and seemed kind. For a long moment, the old man stood there, staring through the crack in the door without saying a word.

The man stared out into the darkness at the visitor standing on his porch, dripping wet in the rain.

Concealed from view, he lowered the sawed-off shotgun that he was holding with the muzzle pressed against the door toward the visitor, setting it against the wall, all while keeping a keen stare on the visitor. He opened the door wide and stepped back.

The first thing James saw was a German shepherd dog standing beside the old man, alert and ready, still as stone, with dark eyes staring. James remained at the doorway, unsure of what to do, wary of the dog, who looked as if he might pounce on him at a moment's command.

"Well, you gonna come in?" the old man's voice was rough and gravelly. "I'm losing heat with this door open."

James stepped inside, keeping a wary eye on the dog still standing there, unmoving. The man closed the door behind him, then moved somewhere off to the side, subtly picking up the shotgun and concealing it somewhere out of sight. The dog barked once; a deep loud bark, the unexpectedness of which made James flinch. It took a step back, lowering its head as it gave a little whine, and then looked back up at James and started panting, now taking a step toward him again.

"Hmph, Huan seems to approve of you. I guess I'll have to heat up some grub. You can warm yourself by the fire."

"Hoo—ahn?" James asked questioningly.

"Yes, Huan the great hound."

James reached out his hand tentatively to let Huan smell him. The dog took a few sniffs and then stepped forward into his hand, allowing James to pet him. "If I can just rest by the fire and warm up for a minute, I'll then be on my way again."

"You look a mess," the man stated matter-of-factly. "Hrmm, I suppose that's to be expected. No respect for the forest anymore, is there Huan? People think they can just come right in with no thought or pretense, wander about carelessly, and then stand there bewildered when they get spat back out." The man was walking about the cabin, moving a few things around here and there and seeming to be talking to himself or the dog as much as to James. "They eventually find out that the forest is not kind or loving, that it will chew them up, grind them down, and stomp them into the dirt." The man now looked at James. "Yes, so it's done with you. Well, you can put some more wood on the fire if you want. I'm sure you're needing to eat."

"Thank you, really. My name's James, by the way."

"I'm Gendry, Thomas Gendry in full, but most folk tend to just stick with Gendry."

"Well, thank you Gendry." James looked around the cabin. He was standing by the door where coats were hung and boots lay on the floor. The cabin was one large room, with flooring of rough-hewn boards and a fireplace against the middle of the back wall, lighting everything in a warm glow. To the right side of the cabin there was a handmade wooden table with two chairs, some cabinets, and a countertop in what the kitchen area must be. To the left there was a bear's head mounted on the wall, its mouth open in a roar, displaying its sharp teeth. Next to this was a bookshelf filled with books, a bed, dresser, and facing toward the fireplace was a very comfortable looking cushioned armchair.

James stopped petting the dog and moved toward the fire, taking off his jacket and reaching his hands toward the flames, trying to warm up. There was a small stack of split wood next to the fireplace, and he placed a few more logs in the fire. James sat down on the floor very close to the fireplace being thankful for whatever brought him to this place. Another day out in those woods and he wasn't sure what state he would be in.

After a short while, Gendry approached from behind James, carrying a cast-iron pot in his hands. "Excuse me, sir." As James moved aside, the man hung the pot on a metal bar that was fastened to the brick fireplace. "You'll have to wait a bit yet, but then, you'll have some of my own almost perfected rabbit stew, which Huan here can attest to as far as its quality, if you have any doubts." The dog licked his chops as he stared at the pot.

It was difficult to remember a better meal than the one he just finished eating. It wasn't so much that the rabbit stew tasted particularly delectable, but with how hungry he was, it seemed to be more fulfilling and satisfying than anything he had eaten before. He set his empty bowl and cup off to the side and reclined on a bear hide a few feet from the fire. James was still planning on leaving the cabin tonight, not wanting to impose on the old man any more than he already had. But as he was lying there, with a full stomach and warmed by the fire, he felt a drowsiness come upon him. He grabbed his backpack and used it as a pillow, faintly aware of Huan licking out the inside of his bowl.

CHAPTER 18

James woke to sunlight shining on his face. He lifted his head off a pillow and looked around, recollecting the features of the cabin. He noticed the blanket covering him and the pillow, which he didn't remember grabbing. Huan was lying near his feet, and Gendry was seated at the table with a steaming cup of coffee, reading a book.

"There's coffee in the pot, and bread on the table," the old man said without looking up from his book.

James patted the dog as he walked over to the table, pouring a cup of coffee, before cutting himself a slice of bread. A small stack of books on the other end of the table caught his attention. The combination of titles stacked on top of each other seemed odd and interesting to James. *Walden Pond* by Henry David Thoreau, *The Silmarillion* by J. R. R. Tolkien, and at the top was *The Holy Bible*, King James Version.

"I think it's time you tell of how you arrived here." Gendry placed the book he had been reading, *A Sand County Almanac* by Aldo Leopold, next to the stack of books on the table.

"Well," James shifted uneasily in his chair, "I was hiking in these woods, and I ended up getting a little lost and eventually ended up stumbling across your cabin. All I need is to be pointed toward the highway again and I'll be on my way. It's highway..."

"Look kid, let's be straight with each other here." The old man gave James a hard stare, and took a moment before continuing, "I live by myself out here in the heart of this forest, out and away from any civilization. I only have Huan here and my books to keep me company, and I seldom have any visitors, never any outsider that got lost on a hike. The sun is only just now rising, and I'm never in a rush out here. I think it's best if you start from the beginning." Gendry took a sip from his mug of coffee.

James let out a heavy sigh. "Maybe that would be for the best after all."

He told his story. Everything that had happened starting with his trip up to Alaska, right up to when he found his way to Gendry's doorstep.

"So now you want to find the girl," Gendry said, more as a statement than a question.

Surprised by the abruptness of the question—or statement—James said, "All I want to know is how to get back to the highway where I left my car."

Gendry closed his book and set it on the table. "When I moved out here and built this cabin, my intention was to remove myself from civilization, from people all together. To pass the rest of my days alone, surrounded by only nature, but the good Lord had other plans for me. As I was building this cabin, I came across some of the people that live nearby. Chloe was one of these people, as were her father and mother, and I came to know her rather well. I visit and trade frequently with both of these differing communities who call this portion of the forest home and retain a good relationship with both parties. For whatever reason—perhaps because I'm an outsider—people like to talk to me, and I have become very familiar with the delicate situation that Chloe finds herself in. I first came here seeking only solitude and peace, but I have come to find community and people that I now consider to be dear friends, and it matters to me what happens between these people."

"All of this is fascinating really, but what does any of it have to do with me? I have nothing to do with these people. I was just supposed to be driving through."

"Supposed to be doing," Gendry muttered. He looked James in the eye. "If it's really true that you care nothing about what happens here, then tell me, why did you run into these woods?"

"Like I said, I thought I saw the girl, Chloe."

"But she means nothing to you, so you've said."

"She doesn't... but I thought she might need some help. It was simply reactionary, and I tried to turn back."

"Very well. I can give you a map that will get you back onto the highway, if that's what you wish. Or, the village isn't far and I could guide you there if you change your mind."

James could hear Elena's voice echoing in his head, *Stop running... find the girl, James.* He took another sip of coffee, and then ran his hand through his hair. "It never ends, does it?" he said, staring into the coffee, his voice barely audible. He looked up at Gendry. "I've heard a lot about this village. Perhaps it's time I check it out myself."

"We better get going, then. The day is waning." The old man got up, and after cleaning off the table, he slung an old-style canvass pack over his shoulders. He waited for James to be ready, and then the three of them were off.

They followed the stream that flowed past the cabin for a short while before branching off, following along a corridor where a dense stand of younger spruce transitioned to mature mixed hardwoods. Walking uphill, they eventually came into a more open area where many of the trees—mostly maple—were large and spaced widely apart.

They traveled mostly in silence, with Gendry making the occasional remark about a tree or plant they passed by. Two or three hours had passed since they had left, and they were now walking along a ridgeline where a view of the mountains could be seen to their left. James noticed a thin column of smoke drifting above the trees, and he knew they must be getting close. He thought he could hear voices in the distance, like some kind of commotion. Then he heard the unmistakable sound of an engine, like that of a vehicle driving by.

They came to a stop at the edge of a rock outcropping, and James could see it all spread out before him, almost feeling like he was being transported back in time. Some three hundred yards out and settled across a sprawling grassy plain below from where they were standing, there was some sort of town or fort, the likes of which he had never seen before in person. A vast wall constructed of many vertical wooden logs which were tapered to a point at the top surrounded a vast series of structures, roads, gardens, and crop fields, which all gave the feel of some ancient and forgotten native village. The structures and buildings found within the walls varied, the larger of which were mostly long and rectangular but with curved roofs bending to the ground like a bow, while most of the smaller structures were either of a more circular and domed appearance or had a squarer form with flatter roofs. Other structures scattered throughout the settlement seemed to hold to altogether different architectural styles and influences. Buildings of similar style and architectural influence seemed to be grouped together, to the extent that the settlement seemed to have very distinct and separate sections within it, giving it a sort of dissonant feel.

Looking down upon the village, he felt a lightness in his limbs, and a warmth rising in his chest. He turned to face Gendry. "Well, I guess this is it then. I am truly grateful for all you've done to help me."

"It was no trouble," Gendry shook his hand, and then called to the dog. "I'm glad that our paths have crossed, and I hope you find what you seek."

"So am I, thank you again." James patted Huan on the head and watched as they both walked back the way they had come.

He went over to the rock outcrop again and looked out toward the village. There was a slight tingling in his skin, and he had an urge to rush forward toward that village. He thought about Sofie, now looking forward to seeing her again, though he wasn't sure what her reaction may be at seeing *him* again.

CHAPTER 19

James found a way down through the trees of the steep and rocky slope, which would then open into the wide green valley he had seen from above. He could hear voices and activity now, which seemed strange as the village should still be some ways away. When James got his first true glimpse of people, it was not at all what he expected.

Approaching the tree line that separated the forest from the clearing, he saw numerous people spread out across a rough line. Some thirty feet out from the forest's edge and running parallel along it, there was a definite path dug into the earth from some sort of bulldozer, which created a low mound of dirt along the side of this path facing the open plain. ATVs and UTVs were scattered about behind this line, and some people were moving large branches and logs, placing them on top of the plowed mound of earth to make what looked to be a kind of barrier or wall. He recalled the sound of the engine he had heard earlier, now concluding that it must have been one of these ATVs. These people did not look like native first nations people, and many of them were carrying weapons, rifles or AR 15s. Also, the barrier of wood and earth was facing toward the village and looked to be in opposition to and not part of that village. He recognized one or two of the people in this group, who James had seen at Gunnar's party. These were his people.

Oh God, what am about to walk into?

James walked past the tree line and approached this semi-barricaded line. One man looked his way, becoming startled when he noticed him, and a flash of recognition came across his face. "Josh?" he called out questioningly. "No, it's Jacob, isn't it? You came in with Ray Neyati, right? I thought you had—I mean, I had heard that you left."

"It's James, actually, but yes, I am the one who came with Ray and the others. Do you know where he is, or Marcos, or any of them?"

"Right, James. Well, Ray should be over there," he pointed down the line, "just keep going until you find a very large tent. Some of the others should be nearby as well. You know, I also need to head that way, so you can just follow me."

They walked along the bulldozed path of bare soil. James looked about at the scattered tents, campfires, and ATVs of different sorts, which occupied the space between this makeshift barrier and the forest. There were people here and there sitting while reading a book or cooking food, or some adding to the wall.

"James?" Marcos was sitting on the ground against a rock busily shuffling a deck of cards when he recognized James walking his way. "Well, I'll be. It is you. I figured you would be across the border by now and halfway to... well, wherever it was you were going. What in all the great white north are you doing here? We all thought you had left?"

James shook his hand after approaching him. "That would be a long story, suffice to say I'm here now."

"Oh, wait... yeah-yeah-yeah, of course! You're here for Sofie, aren't you, you old dog? Decided to take my advice after all and finally make your move on her, huh? Your timing's not great though, you should have acted sooner. Things are rather tense, as you can probably see, but then people tend to exaggerate things—"

"Is she here?" James interrupted. "Do you know where she is?"

"She's not, I'm afraid. Sofie was kind enough to leave us a note, though. It said that she was going off to help Chloe, Gunnar's daughter, as well as trying to help bring about some peaceful resolution to this situation we find ourselves in. We haven't heard from her since. Cell reception the way it is around here makes phones practically useless, so no one knows where she is for sure. We're fairly certain that she must be in the village though, as that's where Chloe went, but it's possible she's still out in the forest somewhere, or even turned back to Gunnar's place." Marcos paused for a moment, then said, "You do know why it is we're all out here, then? I can't really recall what you all know and what you don't."

"I know enough. You mentioned the girl, Chloe. She is here then—In the village, I mean?"

"Yes, she is. We know that much, or at least that's what they're saying."

"Where's Ray? I need to talk to him?"

"Probably still in a meeting, along with Gunnar. They're trying to hash things out with some of the natives from the village."

"Why are *you* guys here, though? I mean, you and Ray and Tehya—I am assuming the whole group is here, minus Sofie, of course? It's just, it looks as if you guys are prepared to go to war, and over what, a weird custody battle between two people, and some timber rights dispute. I can't see what stake you could have in this."

Marcos laughed. "Well, it's a bit more complicated than that. And yes, we're all here." He sat down again, gesturing to James to sit as well. "You see, while Chloe *is* at the heart of this struggle, the reasons for this confrontation between these two groups are much more numerous than just those two issues. We are rather heavily armed, yes, but this is simply a show of strength. We have to appear ready to go to war so that they will agree to our demands. Any chance of a physical display of this force is highly unlikely. 'Speak softly and carry a big stick.' Isn't that what Teddy Roosevelt had said?"

"This is what speaking softly looks like? But sure, it makes enough sense for them, I guess, not for *you*. I don't see what part any of you have in this mess. What do you guys have to do with this first nations group?"

"Gunnar and this group of people following him, they're not just business associates, James, they're our friends, even if we do only see them periodically. Ray especially is a close friend of Gunnar's, and they find themselves in a situation where they could use our help, and so we help them. It's what Ray was talking about before with Machiavelli. Always choose a side. We stick together and stand by our friends out here; it's called loyalty and we are all happy to do what we can. Aside from that, we would also never just leave Sofie here. We're like family, and we never leave family behind. Sofie's out there doing what she thinks is right, for us, Gunnar, and this entire community of people."

"Yeah, okay, I get it," James said, his voice sounding distant. His mind started to trail off as he looked toward the village. All he could see of it from here was the palisade style wall formed by a row of vertical wooden stakes, and a large wooden gate.

Go—find her—make it right, Elena's voice echoed inside of James's head.

Marcos looked at him quizzically. "Are you alright, James? Where have you been, anyhow? I mean, your car was gone so we all just assumed that you had left, but now here you are, what, three days later."

James looked at Marcos. "None of that matters now, I guess." He looked back over toward the village again,

"Hey, let's find the rest of the old gang, huh? Man, they're going to be surprised to see you."

James followed Marcos as he made his way further down the line, greeting a few people along the way, then cut inside, walking past a few trees. Within a small clearing just inside the line of trees where the forest began, there were a few more tents set up. It was here that they found Tehya, Freddy, and Emily, sitting around a campfire, Ray being the only one not there now, besides Sofie.

"No way, hey, hey it's James!" Freddy called out when he saw him.

"Well, well, James Torbour returns. You know I really can't figure you out," Tehya said, and then laughed. "No, really though, we are very happy to have you grace us with your presence once again, whatever the reason may be."

"Well, get over here and have a beer, you son of a gun," Freddy said, as he grabbed one from the cooler, tossing it to him as James walked up.

James sat down between Marcos and Tehya. He greeted them all happily, grabbing some chicken that was still left, which had been grilled over the campfire. They all asked him where he had been and why he was here now. He was thinking about how he should evade their questions, but then he changed his mind.

"Sofie had asked me to help her when she went after Chloe, and instead of helping, I decided to leave. After I left... well, I changed my mind. It's all a bit hard to explain, but suffice to say I came back, and now here I am." It was all that James could bear to say right then, and it *was* mostly true, if perhaps overly brief and lacking in a few details.

They pressed him for more details, but after James evaded their questions the best he could, refusing to mention his time in the forest, they finally got the hint and let it go. Before long, they started to converse and joke with each other like they had before. A smile came to his face as he listened to them, feeling the comfort of being part of this, of being around these people that he could now consider acquaintances, and perhaps even friends. A nagging disquiet remained in the pit of his stomach, however, and as he looked at the flames, he could see her face again, hearing the voice inside his head. *You must leave here, get to the village, find her.*

"James? Earth to James, did you even hear me?" Marcos was saying.

"I'm sorry, but I think it's time for me to leave."

"Really, right now?"

Tehya got up and embraced him in a hug. As she backed away, her hands remained on his shoulders and she looked him in the eyes as she said, "I can see that Ray was right to bring you with us. The fact that you've made your way out here... you are on a path. Now follow it through its course wherever that may lead. You're going into the village, then?"

"I am."

"James, all I ask is that you do talk to their chief, try to get him to lay aside his personal disputes with Gunnar and make peace. Oh, and of course, send our love to Sofie. We're all missing her over here."

James said his goodbyes to the rest of the group, but as he walked away, he couldn't stop thinking about what Tehya said to him, the heartfelt earnestness of her voice.

He walked with a deliberate pace straight toward the gate. He stopped when he was about fifty feet away, unable to see anybody posted along the wall above the gate, or anywhere at all. Everything was still and silent.

"Hey, is anyone there?" James shouted. "My name is James Torbour. I'm a friend of Sofie's and have come to see her." He waited, but there was only silence. "I am unarmed, and I am only here to seek the welfare of my friend Sofie." Still nothing. Minutes passed by as James stood there, and he started to wonder if Sofie even was here; to wonder whether she had ever arrived, or if something had happened to her. He felt a deep pang of guilt once again at not going with her at the start when she asked him.

Finally, the gate creaked open just enough for three men to pass outside. They walked up to James, all of a similar appearance being attired in what appeared to be handmade fabrics, leather, and fur garments. The man in front clearly looked of native first nations descent, as he stood tall with long black hair that was tied back and adorned with several feathers.

It was this man who stopped in front of James and addressed him. "None of our people on watch recognize your face or the name you give, yet you claim to be a friend to Sofie. Tell us how you have come to know her and what brings you from Gunnar's encampment to clamor at our gate."

James cleared his throat. "I have been traveling with Sofie, Ray Neyati, and Tehya, as well as some others down from Whitehorse, and it was then that I became friends with Sofie. Sofie set out to help Chloe and come to this village. She asked me to help her, and now here I am, to help in any way I can. I have no stake in this... disagreement with Gunnar, and do not wish to stir up any further conflict."

The stern man was silent for some time as he stared at James. Finally, he said, "Your story has many unaccounted gaps, yet some truth I can see in it. You can enter our establishment; however, I must state that if you enter, it may be that you will not be able to leave again until this situation is resolved."

"I understand," James said.

"Very well." The man in front gave a signal with his hand to the two other men, who then came forward and one of them frisked James while the other searched through his backpack. "We just have to verify you are unarmed." When they were done, they stepped behind the taller man again. "Follow me then," the tall man stated, and he led James through the gate as the other two followed behind.

James was now walking down a wide dirt path which led straight through the village from the gate. He was constantly looking about to either side of him, which was bordered by gardens of various crops of vegetables—corn, beans, squash, among others—broad-leafed trees scattered about, and wildflowers growing along the path, mostly trillium and bluebells. The dwellings in this part of the village were mostly small and of a round and domed shape, like a wigwam, covered on the outside by sheets of stripped bark or animal hides that were sewn together. There were other people who were walking on the path or working in the various fields and gardens. Down one of the side paths there was a group of children who were kicking a ball around, playing some sort of game. Many of the people he passed by would stop what they were doing and stare at him as he walked by.

As they got deeper into the heart of the village, the architectural style of the buildings changed. The small domiciles he initially passed began to be replaced by long rectangular plank houses, with V-shaped roofs sloping almost to the ground. Wide planks of cedar were used on the rooftop and also formed the siding along the walls.

They halted when they came to a structure unlike any of the others he had seen. It sat mostly beneath the ground, where the only part of the structure visible was the wide, circular sloping roof which met the rising terrain about it. It was built into a slight hill, and the entryway cut right through the ground which sloped up around the structure to meet the roof that was thatched with sheaves of grass and overlaid with bark.

"Wait here, I shouldn't be too long," the man who had been leading the way said, and whom James had now found was named Azaadi, before entering the building.

The two others stayed with James. They sat outside of the structure, and James gazed at the various other buildings that were about him. "How long did it take to build all of this?" he asked the men standing behind him.

One of the men looked at him for a moment and then continued to stare out ahead without answering.

James looked back down the path they had walked up, wondering how all these people came together to live in this way. Did it start out as just a few people and grow from there, or had it been an already established community that came out here and built all this?

Azaadi came out of the structure and again they were walking. They turned off onto a smaller path and came up to one of the larger rectangular buildings built in the style of the Iroquoian longhouse with a sloping arch shaped roof. As they entered, the two men that had been following behind James stayed outside. There were long tables that were strewn across the floor for what appeared to be the drying out and processing of crops. There was a cloth partition that separated this portion of the structure from the back half of the building. This section was one open room with numerous beds placed along either wall, spaced out in a manner resembling a sort of field hospital. Only two of these beds appeared to be occupied, one by a man who was sleeping and had no obvious sign of outward injury, the other by a woman further down toward the back corner of the building. They moved past the sleeping man when Azaadi stopped and gestured toward the woman. There were extensive bandages covering one of her legs, her arm, and most of her torso. James looked at the man and then at the woman, and it wasn't until he started walking up to her that he recognized who she was.

The woman was looking off to the side of her bed, staring at the wall of small logs and thin intertwining branches tied together with rope, imagining images of various landscapes and scenes that those gaps, knots, and shadows might depict, as she had many times since being laid up in this bed. It was only when the footsteps of the visitor got quite close to her that she shifted her body and looked over at who was approaching, wincing momentarily in pain as she did. Her eyes widened as she stared at the man standing above her. "J... James? How—why are you here?"

"Sofie." James drew the name out as he said it, the sound lingering in the still air about them. His lips showed a subtle quiver as he looked over her heavily bandaged right shoulder and left leg. "Sofie, I'm so sorry. How did this—what happened?"

"You know, only this morning I was still cursing your name, yet now that you're inexplicably here, I find myself somehow glad to see your face. Who would've thought, huh? I guess after being confined to this bed for a while, one begins to be grateful for any visitor, regardless of who it may be."

James took a seat next to the bed and took hold of her hand in his, squeezing it tight. A well of emotion rose to the surface as he saw the pain that was evident in her face. "I'm sorry, I... I should've gone with you."

"No shit, James," she let out a derisive laugh— which quickly turned to coughing. "Don't make me laugh. It hurts too much." She gave herself a moment to lie still and let the pain recede again. "A lot of good that revelation does now. But I guess you are here now, for what it's worth. Why are you here?"

"I guess... it's because this is where I'm supposed to be right now."

"Oooh, what an evasive non-answer that is. Whatever the reason, though, I am glad you're here, even though you are a bastard."

James gave an abrupt laugh. "Is that all I am? I figured you might have a few more choice words to sling my way after what you've been through."

"I've called you much worse in my head, don't you worry."

"But really, are you going to tell me what happened, or am I going to have to sit here making up stories in my head?"

"Hey that's a good idea. I should let you sit in ignorance, and just leave you feeling rotten about how you left me on my own like you did. But no, I'll tell you." Sofie recounted the events of finding Chloe, and the encounter with the bear that led to her current state.

CHAPTER 20

James was awakened from the chair he was sitting on by someone shaking his shoulder. He looked up and recognized Azaadi. The man was gesturing for James to follow him. He noticed that his hand was being held by another, and he looked down at Sofie, who was sleeping on her bed, still loosely gripping his hand. He gently pulled it free, being careful not to wake her.

Walking outside of the building, James found it was now dark. Lanterns hung on lampposts spaced at some distance apart, giving only a very modest amount of light to guide the way. They both made their way back to the main road and continued further through the village. James wondered how late it was as he looked up at a star covered sky, partially concealed by scattered clouds. The road was empty save for himself and his guide. They turned off the road onto a narrower pathway and he noticed they were no longer walking on a dirt path, but instead, a well laid out series of flat stones. This continued for a short while, with trees bordering on either side before coming up to a large house flanked by wide overhanging maple and oak trees.

Moonlight shone upon the unique dwelling that James was now gazing upon. A simple square-like structure made up the front of the house, but behind this a two-story structure was built up. It looked similar to the smaller cedar plank house he had seen, the thin cedar planks forming the walls that were placed over the beams which established its structure, and with a V-shaped slanting roof. But it was the multiple glass windows and the height which differentiated it from anything else he had seen in the village.

His guide had stopped just beside the door of this dwelling. "Enter. I will remain out here," Azaadi said as he motioned with his hand toward the door.

James glanced at the man, and then at the door. He moved forward and grasped the doorknob with his hand, hesitating momentarily before opening it. It was dark as he entered the dwelling, but there was a light emanating from the far side opposite him, which beckoned him forward. He passed through some hallway and then again past another room. He stopped in the entryway of a large circular room where a fire was burning brightly in a brick fireplace against the wall. A tall figure stood illuminated in front of the bright flames, with her back toward him, facing the flames to of the fireplace. Long blonde hair tumbled halfway down her back over a simple, light gray dress that flowed down to the ground.

"The hour draws late," the woman said, as she remained staring into the flames. "Aggressors line up at my gate, and every hour that passes draws a war to my city, which becomes ever more impossible to stop with each stroke of the clock. As they line up like wolves feeding ever more on hate, who is there now to stem this tide of madness?"

James stood there. He was about to introduce himself, knowing that he needed to say something, but he remained silent.

"Yet as shadow outstretches its arm, hope still remains. Tell me, James Torbour, why have you come to my city in this late hour?" After she said this, the woman finally turned around to face him. Her complexion was pale and there were faint lines in her face showing her age, but there was a fierceness and beauty to her as she stood gracefully before the fireplace. "Do not be afraid. My daughter has told me of your arrival. Please, take a seat," she gestured to a chair near the fire.

James moved, as if automatically, toward the chair.

The woman moved across the room to a table, pouring a red drink into two glasses from a bottle. She walked over to James, offering him one as she took a seat nearby.

"My name is Isabella. You may know me as the former wife to Gunnar, and Chloe's mother. Negotiations continue to fail; in my dreams, I can see bloodshed close at hand, and now, here one comes alone through my city gates claiming to be a friend to Sofie. I ask again, why have you come here, James?"

James took a sip from the glass, tasting the wine. "Well…" he started, unsure of himself or what he would say, "as you have said, I'm a friend of Sofie, and I came here to find her."

"Chloe has already stated this to me, yet Sofie arrived here days ago. Her friend you may be, but are you not also a friend to Gunnar? We stand on the brink of war. Tell me then why it was not a mistake to let you within the gates of this city?"

It was only now that James sensed that this woman was aware of every movement he had made within these walls, and probably more. "I was asked to help a friend that was in need, and now I have finally come to help in what way I might, though it seems as I have come too late. I have no stake in the other matters that surround you and your… city."

"Ah, but your mere presence implicates you. To help Sofie *is* to implicate yourself in these matters. Now I must ask, are you still willing to help your friend Sofie?"

"You mean... am I willing to help you? That's what you're really asking, isn't it?"

The woman was quiet for a minute, appearing deep in thought. Then she looked up at James again and said, "When you travelled here from Gunnar's place, recall if you will the trees that you passed by, the streams you crossed over, and the rolling hills beneath your feet. Every leaf attached to each tree, a single blade of grass, the dirt and rock underneath, we have just as much right to all of it—no, even more of a right—as any of them. I will not let that man constrain me and my people to the confines of our walls. For that is what he would like, to treat all this land—public land in the eyes of the government—as his own, with no thought for others. The trees know no boundaries, the river is not constrained by the will of man, and a free people will remain free at whatever cost."

Isabella took a sip of her wine, then remained staring at her glass as she continued, "Do not think me ignorant of my part in these matters, however. When I left him, nothing grieved me more than to give up primary custody of Chloe. We didn't go through any court or judicial system, of course. If there is one thing that both Gunnar and I can agree on, it's that we want nothing to do with the government. We handle all our problems and disputes between ourselves out here. Outside law enforcement never gets involved if we can help it. I am the one that left him, I own this, but to see my daughter only periodically, you can't understand how difficult that is. I would kill every single person who stood in the way of me and my dear Chloe if I thought that her wellbeing was at risk. But I do not have the privilege of only acting on behalf of my daughter anymore, as there is now an entire community that looks to me and Kallik for leadership. I will do everything I can for these people, even at the cost of neglecting my own blood."

"There may be something I can do to help in this situation."

"And what would that be? You say you have come here for Sofie. As you can see, she is being well looked after and there is nothing more you can do for her that hasn't already been done. You have seen our village now, and you've looked across the land that is precious to us." Her voice rose and now took on a spiteful edge. "You can't know what I have given up for this city, for these people. I have not suffered these tears and blood only to lose what we have built. We will do anything to protect the way of life we've established here and will not be dictated to by that man or anyone else!" Isabella let out a heavy sigh, and all her anger and heightened animation seemed to evaporate away.

"I'm sorry. I can become passionate when I speak about these things." She stood up and turned to the fireplace. Grabbing the iron poker, she stirred the wood about and put a few more logs on. "War will only destroy us both, as my daughter keeps reminding me. This is why we continue and try to find some common ground with Gunnar and his people. When I look into my daughter's eyes and see the pain and agony that this dispute has caused, this dispute between the people I have been grafted into and the people following her father, it breaks my heart. I question everything I've done. When I see the pain that my decisions have caused her, I am resolved to do anything in my power to fix it. But we continue to fail. We cannot broker a peace that will also retain the rights and freedoms of these people. Gunnar is so blinded by his hate toward me and Kallik that he will not accept any compromise. I understand that it's because of my own actions that have made him so stubborn, but what can I do about that now? I have an entire population that is looking at me to reconcile a dispute which I have in part caused. A population which already doubts and distrusts me because of the paleness of my skin and lack of any first nations blood. Forgive me, you were saying that you could help? Please tell."

James adjusted his position in the chair, running a hand through his hair. His stomach felt like it was all tied up as he looked at the woman who was leaning toward him. "It is my understanding that negotiations between you two are going poorly. I believe I may be in a unique position to negotiate a resolution where others have failed. I think I know what he might accept and how far he could bend in certain areas. If you let me work with you and Kallik, we can work out a new document that is reasonable for both sides. I could then bring it to Gunnar and convince him to accept it. I have his ear. He will listen to me."

Isabella stepped away from the fire and picked up her glass, swirling the red wine about before taking a drink. She straightened her posture, standing tall and elegant. "Perhaps you are right, that you could negotiate this deal successfully. I don't know, it's worth a shot... but there are issues we are not willing to bend on. We shall see. In the morning, we'll talk with Kallik and determine what we can do."

She showed him a cot which was set up on the other end of the room that he could sleep on, and after they moved it closer to the fire, she left to go to bed herself. James lay restless for several hours, having trouble getting to sleep.

Images of dark, swirling water beneath a cliff-side rose to his mind. A dark and foreboding house on a bluff overlooking a picturesque bay. Elena's face looking back at him, sad and full of desperation. Cole Bontone's face shrouded in shadow. A knife's blade—Blood—fire. *No, this time it is different. Something has to change. You have to stop running at some point.*

After dozing in and out several times, he finally noticed daylight streaming into the room. He got up and quietly left the house, walking down the main road as the sun was rising. He went back into the structure where Sofie was, and as he approached her bed, he saw that she was asleep. He quietly grabbed his backpack, which he had left there the day before, and went back outside, sitting down at the base of a tree close to the entrance he came out of. Drinking some water, he sat there contentedly for a while, watching the sun rise over the thatched roofs of various nearby dwellings and at the villagers as they walked by to start their day's work.

He saw a girl that he recognized walking toward the medical building. She glanced in his direction and then stopped as she saw him. She turned and started walking toward him, sitting down in the grass maybe five feet away from him. She was silent for a minute whilst looking at him and then at the surrounding area and sky.

"You know, I saw you yesterday," Chloe finally said. "You were sitting in a chair next to Sofie. You were both sleeping, so I left."

"It's good to see that you're alright, and that you're here," James said.

"I can't help feeling responsible for Sofie's bear attack. I mean, I know it's not my fault, yet it is because of me that she was there when it attacked her."

"I'm sure she doesn't blame you."

"Of course she doesn't. She's a dear friend and I'm lucky to have her in my life."

"I guess I feel guilty about it myself, for my part." James looked at Chloe, who was absently pulling some grass out of the ground. "I'm sorry, I guess I just have to ask and be sure, but it was you that I saw that night on the road when you left Gunnar—your dad's house, wasn't it?"

She raised her eyebrows as she looked up at him, resting her hands on her knees. "Yes, it was."

"Pardon my asking, but why did you run away after I saw you? I called after you. I mean, I was only trying to help... if I could."

There was another pause before Chloe said, "I had heard the collision from the woods, so I ventured onto the road to see what happened. When I saw you, I recognized you from my father's house, and I don't know, I just didn't have time to stop and talk. I was worried that you would try to bring me back to my dad, and I just needed to keep moving, to continue on my course of action. When I heard you following me, I paused and almost went back to find you, but then I felt that our paths were separate, and continued on my way. Yet, it's odd, but sometime later I was somehow sure that you were coming here, and although I thought you would arrive sooner, here you are now."

"Do you know why I've come here?"

"I assume it's to help. Sofie had never mentioned you, but when I saw you at her bedside, I realized that she must have asked you to help her. I don't know why it's taken you so long to arrive, but now that you're here, you better get to work. My mother explained to me how you are in a unique position, being that both she and my father trust you to act with their interest in mind. I don't see that as neutrality myself, but if you're able to get them both to listen to you and agree on a resolution, well, I would like to see that."

"I'll do what I can, but honestly, I'm doubtful it will actually work."

"You're here, aren't you? Of course you'll do everything you can just like Sofie knew you would. I can see that she was right to trust you. I came here trying to find a resolution to this dispute, and well, I've brought my father to the gates of this village and things have finally come to a head." Chloe gave James a weary smile. "I don't know what I expected to happen."

Azaadi, the man who led James through the village the day before, came up to them. "James, I'm sorry to interrupt, but chief Kallik has summoned you."

"Don't worry, I'm sure you'll make a good impression on him. I'll see you around soon. Good luck," Chloe said, walking away toward the medical building.

James followed the man who now led him back to chief Kallik and Isabella's unique cedar plank house. There, Kallik greeted him for the first time. He was tall, broad shouldered, and of a slightly darker skin than most of the other first nations inhabitants, who were mostly not much darker than James himself. Kallik had long black hair that came well past his shoulders with one braid of hair running down his left side that had several feathers tied along it. He was dressed in furs and leathers, but while similar to the garb of the other men in the village, his was of a more colorful and ceremonial in design.

James sat down at a large rectangular dining table opposite Kallik and Isabella. Breakfast was presented, and he heartily ate the eggs, bread, fruit, and coffee that was offered to him.

"Let's get down to it, then. I understand Isabella has explained the situation fully?" Kallik asked when they had finished eating.

"Yes, I believe I grasp the relevant details," James answered.

"Given the brief time that you've had with Gunnar, tell me what you think it will take to get him to back down."

James took a sip of his coffee. "You both seem to look at each other like obstacles that need to be overcome. You are neighbors and should instead be looking at how you can benefit from each other."

"He will not listen, he only has hate for me. Besides, what can he offer us?"

"Medical supplies, bandages, antiseptics, antibiotics, among other things. Is it true that there is a sickness in this village?"

"Hearsay, lies and misinformation spread to weaken our position." Kallik slammed his hand on the table, making the plates and cutlery vibrate. "Gunnar will say or do whatever he can to make us appear weak and vulnerable. You cannot trust the venom that man spits from his mouth."

Isabella placed a hand on Kallik's shoulder. "What my husband means to say is that we are well prepared to deal with any sickness or disease that may currently be spreading through this village without any outside help."

"Even so," James said, "are you really saying that having such medical supplies as these which Gunnar is offering you wouldn't help your people?"

"We have our own ways, our own herbal medications for the ailments we find," Kallik said. "There is such a vast accumulation of knowledge which has been passed down from our ancestors, remedies, and treatments for even the most severe of injuries. We do not need modern medicines. You've seen Sofie, how she is on the mend. All of that was done through our own medicines and the skills of our healers. All without your modern antibiotics."

"I do not mean to criticize your methods or your means, but you can choose to try and benefit from Gunnar and his people, or risk everything you've built to fight against him." James paused, taking a deep breath, and wiping his sweaty palms on the legs of his pants. "Now, getting back to what Gunnar will accept, you are going to have to give in on the forest tenure for logging rights."

"We have tried to compromise on this issue, but he will not budge. He demands that we give him back the tenure for all the lands he previously held. This we cannot do."

James and Kallik went back and forth, arguing and discussing various issues and concerns. As they continued to speak, Kallik eased into a kind, yet authoritative way of speaking that relieved the tension in James's mind and strengthened his confidence in himself. Hours later, they finally came up with a document that listed their new terms for a deal. Kallik handed James the rolled-up sheet of paper tied with a scarlet ribbon.

"I really don't know if Gunnar will agree to this," Kallik said, "but I think this is our last chance to end this peacefully. Don't worry for us if this doesn't work out though, we are fully prepared to defend ourselves if this all goes badly. Isabella never understood why we built a wall around our village, but I think she appreciates it now."

"I just never agreed with the need to wall ourselves away from the rest of nature and the world," Isabella said, moving to Kallik's side. "And when has there ever been a first nations community that has felt the need to do so?"

"We live in a modern world, and we must be ready to defend ourselves with modern methods," Kallik said, giving James a sly smile.

James said his goodbyes and left. Before he was to leave the village, he stopped by the medical building once more. Sofie had her head propped up, reading a book as he walked up to her and settled into the chair at the side of her bed.

She set the book down on the table next to the bed, her movements slow and agitated, before looking over at him.

"So, how are you feeling today?" he asked

"I was just mauled by a bear, James. I can barely move my leg or arm, and even after I drink the concoction of herbs they give me to reduce the pain, my muscles and joints still ache like a dull fire is burning away under my skin."

James looked at the ground. "I... I'm sorry."

"No, no, there'll be none of that now. I'm the one confined to a bed, so I don't need you sulking over the past. I've done enough of that for the both of us, believe me. Chloe told me that you went to speak with Kallik, so tell me, what's the plan?"

"Oh, just trying to negotiate a kind of peace deal. I don't need to bore you with the specifics."

Sofie looked at James with a troubled face before finally replying, "I suppose you're right. There's not much that I can do now, at any rate. I thought I would be able to help her, to assist in bringing about a resolution to this dispute that both parties could agree on. I thought in my own hubris that I could heal the rift within Chloe's family when all I ended up doing was almost getting myself killed by a bear. James, if things do go badly, don't blame yourself. These are good people, both groups. Things like this usually find a way of working themselves out, but in the end, it is their dispute and not yours or mine. Do what you can and leave it at that. Let the rest play out as it will. Don't let the conclusion of this dispute lie heavy upon you."

James sat in quiet contemplation. Then he said, "Don't worry about me, I'll be alright. I better get going, though. I have to talk to Gunnar and try to convince him to accept this deal."

Sofie grabbed his hand. "God's speed James. Do what you can to settle this."

James nodded, and pulling his hand away, he left.

After he had gone, Sofie saw a man who was working on the other side of the building sorting supplies and called him over. "Find Chloe and bring her to me. I need to speak with her."

CHAPTER 21

James walked down the main road through the village. When the gate was in sight, he quickened his pace.

Giving the guard at the gate a written order signed by Kallik which allowed him to leave the village, he exited through the gate and was walking toward the line of people encamped along the tree line. He could feel his heart beating within his chest. External noises around him seemed to dissipate, save for the crunch of grass beneath his feet. The confidence that he felt after talking with Kallik and then Sofie started to sift out of him, but he remained resolute in his course of action and the task before him, pushing all his other fears away.

He thought back to that night, hearing Elena's voice, resolute yet pleading, "Don't forget about me, James." That moment when she brought the knife to her throat. Now a similar circumstance had arrived once more, and somehow people were again seeming to rest their fate upon the actions that he was about to make. Her voice again, "It's up to you, James, to do the right thing." *I will. Your death will not have been in vain.*

Chloe took a seat on the edge of Sofie's bed, anxiously looking at her, wondering why she was summoned.

Sofie propped herself up on the headboard, maneuvering into a slightly more upright position. She took Chloe's hand in her own and said, "I have a bad feeling. Chloe, if things go badly... I think I have an idea, but I'm going to need your help."

There was commotion all along the line where Gunnar's people were entrenched. Someone was yelling, "Form up! Make a line!" People were moving, UTV's were starting up.

As James approached the camp, a man ran toward him. "Hey, hold up there. Who..." he started to say as recognition changed his stern face, "wait, you're that guy with Neyati, James, right? Are you looking to speak with Gunnar, then?"

"Yes, can tell me where he is, I have—"

"You better make it quick. Looks like we're about to head out. He should be by the big tent still," he pointed toward the structure just behind the main line.

James was about to ask what was going on, but the man was already briskly walking away. As James approached the tent, he saw the towering figure of Gunnar standing just outside of the entryway of the tent talking to another man.

"Do what you need to, but get these men up and ready to move. I mean to be leaving within thirty minutes." The man was running down the line as soon as Gunnar had finished talking. "James!" he yelled once he saw him. "Come over here. Tell me, how's my daughter? Is Sofie there as well? I half expected her to be coming back with you?"

"Your daughter is well and trying to do what she can to help end this dispute amicably. Sofie is also there. She was injured while traveling to the village, but she is on the mend and doing as well as can be hoped."

"Well, that is good, I'm sorry to hear about Sofie, you'll have to tell me what happened when we have more time and if I don't hear the tale from her own lips first, but I'm glad that my daughter is safe. We're about to move. Talk has gotten us nowhere and we've been waiting here long enough. Kallik seems to think they are safe behind those walls that they've built, that we lack the fortitude to turn our words to action. We're about to show them how very wrong they are."

When he first approached and saw the uproar along the line, he knew that they were getting ready to move against the village, but James was still shocked to hear it said outright from Gunnar's own lips. Somehow, he never actually thought it would get to this point. He stood there speechless for a moment before remembering why he was there.

"No wait, I talked with Kallik and... Isabella, we have come up with a resolution that I believe will be agreeable to you." James took out the rolled-up scroll and handed it to him. "I think it's something that will be adequate for both parties. If you act with aggression now, it will be too late, and everyone will suffer."

Gunnar sighed impatiently as he took and unrolled the paper and started reading.

After some time, Gunnar rolled the paper back up, tying the scarlet ribbon back around it. "On the surface, these terms are not so unreasonable, but even if I did agree, how can I know that he would follow through on these promises?"

"I've talked with him; he doesn't want a war any more than you do. He understands that he must work with you and not against you. He will abide by the comprises he sets forth."

"Kallik writes that he will withdraw from obtaining the forest tenure logging rights for the first nations people in all but a quarter of the public land where I had previously held them. I would retain logging rights in the other three quarters of that land. He promises that he will notify me of any future prescribed burning they implement and would welcome my participation in it.

Finally, he proposes we establish more robust trade relations in both directions and welcomes a closer working relationship between our two communities." Gunnar tapped the scroll against his hand. "Yes, it would appear to be reasonable, and even though they are still retaining some of the forest tenure for logging, it's something I could live with. But he says he wants to work with me more, establish better trade relations. How can I believe this when I know how he hates me?"

"Because he only wants what's best for his people. He's seen what this feud has done to them, what it's about to do. All he wants is for his people to be able to live free in the way of their ancestors before them. Isabella is the mother of your daughter, and seeing what this has done to Chloe, she is willing to put past grievances aside for her benefit. Why do you think Chloe went over there? She's trying to fix this herself. She's found herself in the middle of this situation, between you and her mother, and all she wants is for the two of you to stop this fighting and animosity between you. Surely it must be worth it to find this peaceful resolution if for no other reason than for her sake."

Gunnar looked off toward the village. "I'll have to see him. I need to look into his eyes and see that he's not lying before I agree to what he's written."

"Of course, that won't be an—"

"Get your hands off me!" a man yelled after exiting the tent nearby. He was dressed in leathers and appeared to be from the village. He yanked away from the grip of one of the men that was leading him away. Catching Gunnar's eye, he yelled, "You seek to ride against us, then? Well good, we welcome you, you've no idea what awaits you behind those walls. This is our land; we will fight for it. You think us weak but have no idea! You're about to see the great strength of the first nations people reawaken again! You—"

"Get that piece of trash out of my sight!" Gunnar roared, "Why is he still here? I want him gone!" The men escorted him away, and he was on his horse, riding toward the village. Gunnar turned to James. "Why would I ever be stupid enough to believe these words? That is the man he sends to negotiate his peace, his 'diplomat' if you will. Lies, all of it lies told to get me off their doorstep. Well, I'll show them both what I think of their deal. Her and that two-faced son of a bitch husband of hers. They're afraid. They realize what I could do to them, so they send me this." He waved the scroll up in the air. "They should be scared. I'll burn their entire village down around them if I have to."

"But..."

"No, the time for words is over. You can either roll with us or walk away." Gunnar brushed past James and started ordering other people around him.

James remained standing there as others rushed about in a frenzy. It almost worked. Gunnar was just about to agree to Kallik's terms for peace, before that man burst out of the tent and riled him up again. He was so close to achieving his part in what Chloe and Sofie had come here to accomplish. James was hardly surprised. There was that one moment when he thought everything was going to work out, but it was shattered as soon as that man started yelling at Gunnar. James still felt committed to be a part of whatever was now about to happen, so he wasn't about to back down and run now. He thought back to when Ray had talked about Machiavelli, and how it was always better to choose a side rather than to remain neutral. He was on a side now, and would see this through to whatever end, remaining loyal to his new friends who had brought him here.

At the stables, Chloe found her mare, which she had named Grey Mist. Her mother had given the horse to her as a birthday gift and taught her to ride. She thought back to that day almost two years ago fondly and only wished she could've visited more frequently. "There you are, girl," Chloe fed her a carrot as she stroked the side of her neck. "It appears we might have a task to accomplish if we can. I know I can count on you, Mist."

She saddled the horse and was soon moving through the village at a quick walk. When she approached the gate, she noticed a wagon that was parked next to the stairs leading to the top of the wall. A man standing on top of numerous boxes was... she moved closer and got a better look. She saw the man on the wagon handing modern day assault rifles up to another man, passing them along to the people stationed on the wall.

No-no-no-no, this isn't good; this isn't good at all. She approached the guards at the gate and demanded to be let out. They refused, stating that they were commanded to keep the gate closed at this time.

"I'm on an urgent mission from chief Kallik himself and I must be allowed to leave," Chloe shouted authoritatively from atop her horse, thinking how it was only half a lie after all. The guards still refused. "Do I have to go and fetch the chief away from his busy tasks and watch him bash your heads together for not obeying his direct order? Don't you know who I am? Now open the door!"

"No, I mean yes m'lady, of course," the guard at the gate fumbled, "We'll get the door open right away, meaning no disrespect. Just following orders, miss, you understand."

Chloe silently thanked God when the gate opened. A slight shakiness in her hands and brief tremor in her voice were the only outward indication she showed of the nervousness she felt. Inside, her heart was racing, and she felt sticky with sweat. She flicked the reins and galloped out into the open plain.

Everyone had lined up now, with Gunnar and about ten others around him on horses, whilst everyone else was in UTV's, some fifty of them in a line. There had to be well over a hundred people all together. It seemed so surreal to James as he looked about on either side. He had found Ray and the rest of the group and was now seated next to Marcos, who was unusually quiet. They had moved in a line halfway across the plain toward the village walls before stopping. Another UTV had moved out in front of the line now. There seemed to be no one driving it, and something was packed into the driver and passenger seats of the vehicle. James was near the center of the line, not too far from where Gunnar was. Everything had now grown quiet, and he could hear Gunnar talking to someone else.

"Drive the package straight for the gate and then detonate."

"Shit, James, that thing over there's a bomb," Marcos said as he sat next to him.

A man next to Gunnar was holding a controller and appeared to be operating the vehicle remotely. The vehicle with the bomb was moving again, picking up speed as it raced toward the gate.

"A rider? Yes, I can see him," Gunnar said, talking to the man next to him. "Why would they be sending out a rider now? Kallik must know it's too late for that."

Chloe saw the UTV heading toward her, wondering what her father could be doing. She forced herself not to diverge from her path as she passed the driverless vehicle, seeing the explosives. "Oh fuck. I can still stop this—I can still stop this. Please let me be able to stop this."

"That's not a rider, that's a girl. That's my Chloe—what in hell is she doing?" Gunnar said. The girl was now only about twenty yards from them. "Wait—no—the bomb. Hold up, don't detonate—"

An explosion rocked the ground as Gunnar was still talking. Flames shot up thirty feet, rising above the top of the wall as the gate shattered into pieces, scattering chunks of wood big and small, along with burning embers across the vicinity.

"No!" Chloe shrieked as she looked back at the explosion. Looking forward again, she rode to where her father was. "What have you done, Father?" She could feel the adrenaline and fear in her veins.

"I am doing what is necessary. They will surely surrender now, knowing what we are capable of. What are you doing out here? It isn't safe?"

"No, you don't understand. You must turn back and hope it isn't too late." Chloe was becoming frantic as she hurriedly glanced about her. Her horse taking a few steps in one direction and then another, sensing the anxiety of its rider. "They have guns. All of them, the walls are lined with assault rifles. They will cut you down before you even reach the walls." She looked back, wondering if they were even now far enough away, worrying that at any moment they might open fire upon them.

"What? This is nonsense. You're hysterical Chloe, you don't know what you're talking about. They adhere to the old ways of bow and spear and would not have modern munitions. Surely you're mistaken."

"I've seen them. I've seen them with my own eyes and I'm telling you, if you move on that village you will die." She looked at her father, who was now staring out at the smoldering gate. "You must believe me, Father."

Gunnar got off his horse and walked toward her. She got down to the ground and was immediately embraced by Gunnar.

"Yes, of course I believe you, Chloe. Are *you* okay? You're not hurt or anything, are you?"

Chloe pulled away from him just enough to look him in the face. Tears were in her eyes and smeared across her cheek. "I'm okay, Father, I am... but I love my mother as well. You must make peace with her; you have to make this right. They really aren't that different from us, you know; they just want to have the freedom to live their lives as they feel fit, just like we do. Please don't go to war Daddy, I love both of you. I love both you and Mother. I don't want to see you fight like this; I can't take it anymore."

"Shh, Chloe, it will be okay," he pressed her head to his chest. "You're right, my dear, you're right. This is not the way. I will broker a peace agreement yet, I promise you, I'll make this right."

A moment passed and then his right-hand man spoke up and said, "Uh, Gunnar, sorry, but there's a lot of smoke rising from behind the walls. I think some of the buildings inside may have caught fire."

Gunnar looked up and saw the smoke rising. He got back onto his horse and asked for some white fabric. One of his riders took off his white tee-shirt he had on underneath his jacket. Gunnar tied it onto a pole, and then said, "I will take two other riders with me initially, as well as my daughter. We are going to help them extinguish any fires that may be burning. Once we enter the gates, the rest of the riders on horseback can follow. We can come in ten by tens after that and we will all be completely unarmed as we enter. Leave your weapons here. We don't want to give them cause to shoot at us as we enter, so we will go in as small groups, and I will talk to them when I enter. If they forbid any of you from entering, listen to them. Now let us ride and not waste any more time. We must do whatever we can to help them as we have caused this fire." With that, they rode off.

For a while, they only let the ten men who were on horseback through the gates. Twenty or so others of whom James was a part of got out of their vehicles, and after disarming themselves walked up to the gates. There was wooden debris scattered across the ground, some of which were still smoking and smoldering as they walked up to the wide opening in the wall where the gate once was. What little fire which had caught in amongst the timber of the wall itself had been quickly put out shortly after the explosion, and now there was only the blackened char that remained and some lingering smoke. Most of the smoke, which was still pouring into the sky, was coming from inside the walls. Two men were standing just outside of the absent gate and were carrying what looked to be AR-15's of some kind and stopped them. They wouldn't let anyone else inside and remained silent when asked why or about what was going on behind those walls.

James, along with Marcos and the rest of the twenty people in the group, sat on the ground and waited. It was about an hour later when James looked up and saw Azaadi walking out toward them with another man near his side.

"You all," Azaadi said, addressing the group, "You can follow me inside. The rest," he gestured toward the rest of their people who had remained with the vehicles and equipment in the field, "they must remain out here."

They sent one runner back out to the main party in the field to inform them of what was going on while the rest of the smaller group by the gate entered the village. Immediately off to their left upon entering within the walls, was a smoking heap of collapsed timbers and wreckage still mildly burning away, the remains of a small dwelling or perhaps a gatehouse. As they continued down the path, there were two more buildings adjacent to the first, which were in a similar state of burned wreckage. Many men, women, and children were standing along this road staring at them as they walked by, some with a vacant look in their eyes, some weeping, and others with clear expressions of stark hostility and anger. After passing the third burned down structure, there was another long building positioned slightly further away. This one was still standing and on top of its roof there were many blankets which had been soaked with water and thrown over the top. One corner of the building was deeply charred by fire, but it seemed that they had extinguished the fire before it spread too far.

James was later told what had happened after Gunnar and a few of his men entered the village. How the first building was already engulfed in flames as they entered, and the second building had just caught fire. There was a stream which flowed through the middle of the village, and it was from this source that many people were already hauling from, using buckets and jars and whatever other implements which could hold liquid they could find and then ran toward the flames with it. Kallik and Isabella were there directing people in what to do, and after a brief discussion with them, Gunnar and the others fell into the line that was formed of people heading to the stream and then back to the fire. By the time there was a steady line of people laden with water heading back to where the fires were burning, the second structure had been completely engulfed in flames, and after dumping some water on the third building which was also well on fire, they deemed it was a lost cause and instead focused on the fourth. A corner of that building had caught fire as well as the roof, but they had intervened in time to where they were able to douse the flames with water. Several people had caught on to how the thatching and bark of the roofs was catching fire and brought soaking wet blankets to drape over it and wet it down. The roofs of several other surrounding buildings had caught aflame from the falling embers, but by this time, there were plenty of people around, ready with water to douse the flames before it spread anywhere.

The fires had been stopped, and it seemed that the open hostility and impending bloodshed between these groups had also been suppressed, at least for the moment. As James was looking around, he saw Gunnar and Kallik walking up to them side by side, both of them dirty with black soot on their clothing and faces. They were talking to each other as they walked. Gunnar patted Kallik on the back and smiled over something that he had said.

Epilogue

2 WEEKS LATER

"How much farther is it? I mean, I know I'm making it look easy, but walking through these woods in crutches is actually a real pain." Sofie paused in her stride, sweat dripping down her face as she looked at James just ahead of her. Breathing heavily, she adjusted her one good foot into a more comfortable standing position. Her other foot and entire leg were wrapped in bandages and a makeshift splint formed by two planed boards rigidly tied to both sides of her leg, holding it immobile.

"Hey, you're the one who was complaining about still being stuck in that village. Now that you get your wish, you can do nothing but complain," James said.

"Yeah, well, let's see a bear take a sizable chunk out of your leg and see how chipper you are after walking miles through the woods."

"Oh, it hasn't even been a half-mile, but it isn't far now, really. I discovered this spot while wandering around a few days ago. Trust me, it will be worth it when we get there."

With a sigh, Sofie reluctantly resumed moving forward once again, following James as he led her over a rather indistinct path through the open woods. They were going uphill now, which made the pace even slower, but she persevered through the pain and exhaustion. Soon the slope leveled off and she could see a vast open space through the trees ahead. "And I thought the drive in the UTV across the valley getting to this trail was bad. I think I like this walking business even less, James."

"Hey, we're here."

They walked to the edge of the tree line and found themselves on top of a rocky bluff that dropped off steeply in front of them. Down at the bottom of this bluff stretched a forested valley with a wide river winding through the center of it. Beyond this, the forest rose again into the mountains, which towered on the other side.

James helped Sofie as she sat on a large rock. They looked out upon the picturesque view that stretched out before them, sitting in silence like this for several minutes. Sofie pulled a pack of cigarettes out of her pocket, taking one out and placing it between her lips. She gestured the pack toward James, holding it out to him for a moment as he declined before placing it back in her pocket, a smile forming on her lips as she did.

Exhaling her first puff with a sigh, she looked up past the tops of the mountains. "This is good, isn't it?" She said it more as a statement than a question.

James stayed quiet for a moment before saying, "I'm leaving tomorrow."

Sofie looked at him. "That's good. You must be looking forward to finally getting home?"

"I think that's where my road is finally leading me back to, yes. I do have to straighten a few things out with the law regarding what had happened in Alaska. A detective up there had been calling me, and now that I've had some time to breathe and think, I've finally called him back. There are some things I need to explain, and I'll be meeting with a colleague of his when I get into Washington. I was involved with something that happened after Elena's death that I could be charged with, but it sounds like everything could still work out alright."

"Whatever had happened, I hope you're right, that it will work out. Regardless of all that, I'm glad you stayed here to see everything through."

"Yeah, although I still feel like I did little myself to resolve things."

"You were here, standing by your friends and doing what you could. I would say that's as much as any of us can do. All I managed to do was to get attacked by a bear, so..."

"You were standing by Chloe when no one else was. And you didn't let the bear defeat you."

Sofie laughed. "Not through any act of my own."

"I mean your attitude after the event. Like look at you now."

"Oh sure, I'm a real glass half full kind of cripple."

"Do they know how long it will be before you can fully walk on it again?"

"Not sure, a couple weeks at least yet. Ray thinks I should go to a proper hospital, somewhere where I can get x-rays and more *expert* help and all that. But Kallik and his people have given me excellent care here, and I seem to be recovering alright. I don't know, maybe he's right and I should go somewhere else. I do like it here though. It's nice to just be away from everything, you know."

"And Ray and Tehya will continue to wait until you're ready to leave."

"For sure, they're happy to stay here for some time yet, and don't have anywhere else they need to be right now. With Marcos, Freddy, and Emily already gone and now you leaving, it will be nice to still have Ray and

Tehya around. Now that things have settled down around here, with Gunnar and Kallik both agreeing to terms they can both live with, it's quite peaceful and nice around here. It's also rather fascinating to see how these people are living."

James looked out into the vast country out in front of them as they both stayed silent for a minute.

Sofie took a last draw from her cigarette before snubbing the butt out on a rock. "So, what about you then, James? Are you good?"

James could feel her staring at him without having to glance over at her. He continued looking forward across the valley when he finally answered, "Well, not really." He then looked over at her with a faint smile and said, "But I now know that I will be."

Sofie was smoking another cigarette as she repositioned herself into a more comfortable position against the rock she was sitting against.

"What are you going to do?" James asked. "I mean, when you're able to leave here, where are you going to go, back to Whitehorse?"

"After everything that's happened, I don't know. I've just really started to miss home. I'll stay with Ray and Tehya for a bit, but then I think I'm going to move back to Norway."

"Home." James said it as if to himself. "Yes, that is good. I'm sure you will find your path there. You know, I am glad to have been able to know you, even if only for this short time."

They continued to sit in silence again until the sun had gotten noticeably lower. "This has been really nice," Sofie finally said. "I suppose, though, it's getting late, and we probably should start heading back,"

"Yes, I suppose we should." James helped Sofie get to her feet, and they walked back into the forest as the sun waned in the western sky.

"You know this is going to take a while, having to put up with me slowly staggering my way back to the UTV with this leg."

"Are you kidding? That's the reason I brought you along. There're bears out here, and this way if one attacks, I can just run clear and leave him with you."

"Oh, is that right, huh? Let him finish what his cousin started while you stay free and clear."

"Well yeah, I mean the bear's cousin—or brother— or second aunt; they're all going to be out looking for *you* anyway, seeking their revenge."

"So that's all I am, easy prey in case of an attack."

"Hey, it's a dangerous world out here. One has to take precautions."

"Well, just because I can't run, doesn't mean that I can't take you out before you do. I'll just jump toward you, take you down, smash *your* knee and then hobble away while the bear feasts on your leg."

"Well, I guess I better watch my back then. Who knows what you might try?"

"Oh, you better, mister. I'm like an animal, even more dangerous when I'm wounded."

Intermittent laughter drifted through the trees as they continued this banter, slowly making their way back to the village.

ACKNOWLEDGMENTS

I would like to thank my editor, Shelley Routledge, for all the input and corrections she made to help form this book into the polished and cohesive work that it now is.

Also to Ray Braun and Vicki Neighbours for their work with the final proofreading. And to Claire with Damonza for making the cover art.

A special thanks to both my parents for their input on the story and to everyone else who had some form of impact on this book being written and completed.